From the Foot of the Mountain

From
the Foot
of the Mountain

by
Claudia Morrison

Cormorant Books

The publisher wishes to thank The Canada Council
and the Ontario Arts Council for their support.

Cover froman etching and silkscreen
by James Boyd entitled *The Secret of the Space Ship*,
courtesy of the artist and The Canada Council Art Bank.

Published by Cormorant Books,
RR 1, Dunvegan, Ontario, Canada K0C 1J0

Printed and bound in Canada
by Hignell Printing Limited in Winnipeg, Manitoba.

Canadian Cataloguing in Publication Data

Morrison, Claudia, 1936-

From the foot of the mountain

ISBN 0-920953-43-3 (bound). -
ISBN 0-920953-33-6 (pbk.)

I. Title.

PS8576.07425F76 1990   C813'. 54   C90-090406-2
PR9199. 3 .M67F76 1990

To My Daughters

...In the Ninth Year of the Emperor Vespasian

10 June

I take up the pen at the recommendation of Eutarchus, our family physician, whose prescribed therapy I have agreed to follow—herbs, massage and careful diet for my body, and a program of study and writing for my mind. I am to review the major works of our philosophers and keep a daily journal of my reflections. According to him the act of setting out my thoughts in writing will cure the melancholy I have been suffering, enabling me to gain greater objectivity and clarity of mind. I must make new resolutions, he says, chief of which must be to eschew all habits and behavior that have contributed to my illness. Only thus, I am counselled, will I ever achieve harmony and peace.

A few days ago my depressed states of mind became so severe I made the decision to terminate my life. I summoned Eutarchus to my rooms and asked if he would instruct me in the least painful method of opening my veins and whether he would consent to assist in the act. Although I offered to pay him well for such service, he refused. Instead he insisted upon an immediate consultation, and after examining me physically and verbally for an entire afternoon, persuaded me that my original belief, namely that suicide in our philosophy is considered a

7

moral good, was seriously in error. The choice of death by one's own hand was permissible only when honour had been irredeemably damaged, I was told, or life rendered intolerable. Neither could obtain in my case, for there was no dishonour involved; the suffering I was presently experiencing was temporary and amenable to treatment. He chided me for not coming to him sooner and pleaded with me earnestly to put any thought of death from my mind. For the next six months I am to follow the therapeutic course he has outlined.

I expressed doubt that the perusal of philososphy would relieve my gloom, adding that I thought it would more probably intensify it, but I was assured that the opposite was true. "The world becomes clear when it is seen in its fullness, both in time and space," he said, "but only to an eye schooled in Reason and a Will trained to obedience."

I felt as if I was being sent back to school, made once more a child. "Am I to confine myself in my writing then solely to learned matters," I asked, "to copying quotations from our thinkers?"

He bowed in denial and informed me that the record of my self-examination should reflect whatever engaged my soul. "If grief is what you feel at the time speak of that," he said, "and accord it due attention. The same is true for your joys. The stylus should move where the spirit enjoins, even if the journey is into apparent confusion and inconsequence. To become one with the *logos* one must first know it as it appears in its original shape, which according to our philosophy is Chaos."

I find Eutarchus wearisome and sententious at times, but in spite of my skepticism I was intrigued, for it was not the advice I expected. "Surely," I objected, "it is necessary in writing to order one's thoughts."

He agreed but counselled me not to despise disorder on that account. "Reject nothing in advance as trivial,"

8

he admonished, "nor dismiss an idea because it violates the canons of virtue or taste. To do so is to exercise a premature censorship and confine yourself too narrowly."

He further surprised me by advising me to pay attention to my dreams, which have given me much trouble of late, explaining that it is in disordered, nocturnal states of mind that we encounter the voice of our *daemon*, our deepest, most hidden self. "It is an error to dismiss this voice," he warned. "It must be confronted and understood if we wish to diminish its negative effects and incorporate its strengths into our characters. Write, dear lady, write."

I have little faith in the healing properties of his prescription, and shall perform the exercise largely to avoid displeasing him. He is a good physician, if slightly absurd in his pretentions, and presumably three fifths of any cure is faith in one's healer. But I fear that the reverse of his intention is more likely to result from his proposed course of therapy: that instead of finding relief from pain through expressing my thoughts in writing I shall be driven more deeply into it and my original purpose confirmed. I doubt, you see, that disorder can be turned into form or suffering transmuted to acceptance, as our good philosophers claim.

Nevertheless, I obey. I begin.

* * * * *

I became afflicted with my present melancholia some six months ago, shortly after the night my son Drusus coughed up quantities of blood and fell into a deep trance. Convinced he was dying, I prayed to the gods to spare him, offering to substitute my life for his. My prayers were granted. He is much improved now, although his convalescence will be long.

You would think that when the danger was over

my spirits would have lightened, but it was not so. If anything, my condition is worse now than it was then. I continue to perform my duties, I have not taken to my bed, but my nights are filled with oppressive dreams that are far more vivid than the stuporous days that seem to drift past unconsidered and unlived. It is as if I have been robbed of all capacity to feel. Even pain now is dull and far off, swallowed up in a dark, unreal cloud. The only sensation I experience is a feeling of being unmoored. I am disconnected from my surroundings, disconnected particularly from those I love.

Propertius, Lucilla, even Drusus, seem to me one-dimensional and remote: alien beings for whom I feel nothing. Increasingly I see Propertius, kind as he is, as a pathetic, aging stranger, enslaved to his devotion to work. As a husband and as a citizen he is exemplary, which is to say he performs his roles with perfect correctness, yet I have perversely come to feel contempt for every one of his virtues.

No, not I, properly speaking: it is that other creature inside me that thinks this way. It is she who dislikes Propertius, who calls his patience pomposity and insinuates the thought that his life is nothing but a composite of empty gestures.

I have striven to silence this voice. Outwardly I remain as loyal and dutiful as I have through the twenty years of our marriage. I do penance to the gods whenever I feel this other personality taking hold, spinning yarn for long hours with the women in the slave quarter in order to quench it. But I do not succeed: the voice is not silenced.

It is as if I have constructed a wall around myself that I feel powerless to dismantle. I do not think I even desire to any longer, any more than I desire to make love to Propertius.

It is odd that that comparison should occur to me. It is five years since Propertius has come to my bed: his impotence must be confirmed by now. I often wonder how much I contributed to the condition by recoiling from him; perhaps I should have been more patient. It was intermittent at first, and he insisted on giving me pleasure manually even if he experienced none himself, but although I achieved release through this practice, I could not escape a feeling of degradation afterward which made our relations repellent. I ceased encouraging him and gradually, without speaking of it, touch between us became a thing of the past.

My love for my daughter Lucilla has also quite dissipated. Even before her marriage last year, I had come to see her as despicably shallow. The cold emptiness beneath the coquettish airs I found so charming when she was young revealed itself to me with appalling clarity. I can detect no goodness in her character, only a fertile field for corruption. I have found myself thinking many times that it was not worth the time and effort to have given birth to her, yet even this thought, which would earlier have shamed me, I privately greet with indifference.

What I have left of shame is reserved for the dearth of feeling that exists now between myself and Drusus. Increasingly I can scarcely bear to be near him; I have to force myself through our daily encounters, my veins turning to ice as the occasion approaches. He senses this, I am sure, no matter how I try to disguise it, and is deeply bewildered. He has become increasingly respectful and polite, his approaches more ritualistic than sincere, as if the burden of our duplicity has stiffened us both into unnatural postures, making our times together awkward and strained.

Propertius has hired him a new tutor, a young freedman from Rome by the name of Camillus, who should be here within the week. Drusus is very excited at the prospect of his coming. I too look forward to it, for it will relieve me of a strain I feel progressively unable to bear. I

11

pray this man will develop a bond with Drusus, that he will serve for him as a model and source of esteem that will compensate for my failure to provide either.

O my son, my son, forgive me for having turned away.

June 11

What precipitated my sickness was an instant of revelation that occurred shortly after the crisis with Drusus had passed and I knew that my prayers for his life had been answered. At first I experienced joy, relief, gratitude. But a few days later, as I was sitting in the garden thinking back on what had occurred, I was struck by how absurdly fragile human happiness is, and how completely and unthinkingly dependent we are on others. Looking back on my life, it seemed to me I had been living in a theatre of illusion. At any time, and without warning, the gods could suddenly, violently, alter the script. True, they had saved my son, but it was only a reprieve, a whimsical respite: the power remained in their hands at any instant to snatch him from me, which they would do, I was convinced, whenever it suited their fancy. It was clear to me that no action of mine could in any way alter this fact.

I do not quite know why, but this simple perception of how easily one can be robbed of what one loves by death precipitated me into a state of depression that has lasted since then, unreprieved. During this time I have increasingly withdrawn from social intercourse and confined myself to our home. I spend long hours in my rooms doing nothing, or wandering aimlessly in the garden, like some demented Ariadne who has lost the thread, wandering in a labyrinth from which there is no exit.

It is as if everything gave way with the realization that Drusus could be taken from me with no more explana-

tion or concern than I would give to crushing an insect—
and with even less justice, for insects meet their deaths at
our hands because they have annoyed us, whereas Drusus
is surely no bother to the gods. It seemed obvious that not
justice but chance ruled our lives. At a stroke I was bereft
of belief; my love of my family, my respect for virtue,
seemed to vanish into a void. Everything was reduced to
nonsense and mockery, and the motive springs of action
broken.

Eutarchus tells me that such an experience is not
uncommon but that it normally passes with proper rest. I
experienced something similar years ago when my father
died, but my response then was covered over with numb-
ness and childish denial. It is as if my recent grief over
Drusus tore open that older wound, which had never been
allowed to bleed. I feel it throbbing inside me now continuously, as if my life blood secretly beats to its rhythm.

Eutarchus wishes me to think that my depressions
are a product of ill health and false reasoning, that the way
I see the world in my melancholia is a delusion of truth and
not the thing itself. It may be so. The very fact that I have
consented to his therapy would seem evidence of some
kind of a renewal of will, that somewhere within me the
desire to live is once again stirring.

In any case, I shall go through the motions. I am
to begin my visits to Stabiae Friday, to the villa of Pomponius. Eutarchus, who is physician to Pomponius' family as
well as our own, has arranged that the library there will be
opened to me. I am to spend one afternoon a week in
study. I am assured I shall meet no one and shall not be
disturbed: the villa is used by the family only during the
winter months, so aside from the slaves, it will be unoccu-
pied. Even so I find the prospect frightening, for I have not
left our grounds since my spells of melancholy began.

I blame my dreams for this fear. Always when I
dream of being outside these walls I encounter some

terrible disaster. When Propertius and I came here seventeen years ago it was months after the great earthquake, yet I still remember my shock at seeing the extensiveness of the damage. Propertius says my nightmares represent my fear of another such occurrence, and perhaps they do. But in all these years the ground beneath us has shown no signs of disquiet; I do not understand why I should be having such dreams at this particular time, nor why they present themselves with such compelling certainty.

Whatever their cause, my fears will have to be suffered; the will must be summoned, in alliance with whatever faith I can call upon. It is selfish to long for death: for Drusus' sake, I will keep my compact.

June 13

The visit to Stabiae, which I had looked forward to with trepidation, turned out to be a day of renewal and discovery. It began badly, with me huddling inside the litter refusing to look out the curtains. When I stepped down on the quai and into the boat I was actually shaking with fear, but once settled against the cushions the anxiety eased. The beauty of the day forbade it. In the bright sunshine the water surrounding us was a deep aquamarine, as calm and reassuring as a nurse. A few large stationary clouds dominated the sky; the sunlight played on the walls of the buildings on shore, making them dance with colour and shadow. Why have I not come here before, I almost cried out, amazed that for so many months I had denied myself such beauty.

My fear of the sea seemed inexplicable, impossible to fathom on such a day. The oarsmen rowed, Scamander leading them. I relaxed against the cushions, drinking in the air and the tang of the sea spray, allowing myself to be lulled by the gentle rocking motion of the boat. It was a

14

rare experience for me to feel so calm and buoyant on water, so unexpectedly full of trust. It was as if without my knowing it my eyes had hungered for the continually changing spectacle of this coast, where each new alteration in the angle of vision brings fresh joy to the senses.

The voyage seemed surprisingly brief; too soon we were mooring at Pomponius' dock. Scamander moved to set up my litter, but I motioned him away. The series of stone steps leading up to the villa promised pleasures of its own. I would walk.

The path was shaded by plane trees and tall boxed hedges through which was entwined a lovely species of ivy, its leaves so deep green in colour their polished surfaces reflected back shimmers of light. The villa itself is a place of great elegance, with a commanding view of the bay and the coast. It is extremely large and clearly very costly, but without the showy ostentation that is the mark of seaside retreats such as this. The rooms are simple but composed with obvious care. The wall paintings in particular are of great delicacy, some in the ornamental style, some in the illusionist. The latter I found especially attractive, both in the central dining hall and in the baths.

In the triclinium, the panels are done in an intricate design of trees and peacocks against a deep blue background. The brush work is exquisite, the effect dreamlike. There were also four full-length panels depicting mythological scenes. I was particularly struck by one portraying Perseus' rescue of Andromeda. It is large, covering the entire wall. Andromeda stands chained to a rock while below her nymphs are bathing in a pool. Behind there are buildings, shapes of trees; in the extreme foreground a delicate rendering of birds and small animals gazing at their captive princess with longing and grief. The panel is framed in deep red; inside it soft blues and greens predominate, except for the splash of matching red that comprises Perseus' cloak. The eye is drawn by this colour to his

15

small figure far off in the distance, where he can be made out flying to Andromeda's rescue. The design and conception are enchanting; I long to know who the artist was.

I was shown through the villa and gardens by a pretty young slave who gave her name as Brytha. Pomponius' wife must be very confident of her own beauty to have in the house so tempting a creature as this, I thought, and wondered what country she was from. Perhaps from Hibernia: I hear the women there are uniformly handsome, with the same golden-reddish hair.

After we completed the tour, she led me to the library and discreetly left me. The room was all one could wish for, a place of calm and order. All four walls held rows of shelves, each filled with neatly tagged scrolls. Such a great quantity of writing! Eutarchus had told me the library held two thousand works, but I had not been able to picture it. Drama, Poetry, History, Law, Philosophy—all were there in abundance. I moved to the shelves beneath the portrait bust of Aristotle and easily found what I was looking for. Eutarchus had advised me to start with the works of Lucretius and progress from there to Epictetus and Epicurus if Lucretius alone did not provide the answers I sought. I chose therefore Books I through III of *On The Nature of Things* and carried them to the writing couch beside the window, prepared to settle in to my task. But the room itself, so perfectly ordered for study and contemplation, distracted me. I found myself delighting simply in the sensation of being there, being part of the quiet light and the rich woods, the almost holy aura that emanates from rows of ordered shelves surmounted by busts of revered thinkers. The old tantalizing call of knowledge that I remember from my girlhood re-awakened and stirred. I gazed at the mural on the opposite wall. It was a portrait of Socrates in prison surrounded by his followers, holding the cup of hemlock before his lips. How can the heart not be gladdened by reminders of such noble souls? Voices seemed to breathe from the shelves, stilling the clamor of the outside world, its follies, its cruelties, its wretched, purposeless suffering. I held the chosen scroll in my hand, savoring its promise.

But in an instant, and for no apparent reason, I was overtaken with bitterness. I castigated myself for being so pliant, so uncertain and wavering of mind that I continually allowed myself to be seduced by the vain, soothing prescriptions of men. Who was Eutarchus, even Lucretius, that I should listen to them rather than the voice of my own heart? Within minutes I was plunged again into melancholy, as suddenly as if someone had blown out a candle. The room that had offered such pleasure a moment before now seemed oppressive, the pursuit of philosophy yet another contemptible temptation to illusion. I left and went outside.

The courtyard is a long rectangle, in the center of which there is a fountain surrounded by a circular pool. Flowering bushes alternate with benches and porticos, offering patches of cooling shade. Beyond them cypress trees are silhouetted against the hills, and beyond that one can see the bay sparkling in the distance.

At the far end of the courtyard I was surprised to discover a small columned sanctuary. Surely that is a shrine to Isis, I thought, and approached to examine it more closely. The statue between the columns was indeed Isis, seated on a throne with the infant Horus in her arms, her foot resting on the globed earth. Mother of All Things her devotees call her, Goddess of Many Names: Cybele in Thrace, in Sumeria, Ishtar. I understand the cult is finding increasing favor with the masses in all parts of the empire, even in the capital. What surprised me was to find it here: the worship of Isis is unusual among the patrician class, or so I have been led to believe.

I know from Eutarchus that Pomponius is a Senator and former consul. I wonder what his wife's background is. Clio: the name is Greek. I presume it was she who erected this elegant shrine.

I resumed my seat by the fountain, my melancholy somewhat relieved. I reminded myself that the decision to discipline my mind through study was after all something I had agreed to, that resistance was childish and self-destructive. I dutifully opened the scroll, but my thoughts refused to obey my commands and slipped off on paths of their own. It occurred to me that perhaps the cure Eutarchus had in mind would proceed as much from the villa itself and its soothing view as from study. Perhaps the idea of reading philosophy was only his lure, I thought, and I was meant really to bask in the garden, under pretense of perusing Lucretius. I found it increasingly difficult to concentrate. The warmth, the heavily perfumed air, the droning murmur of the insects mingled with the soft plash of the fountain made me drowsy. Briefly I slept, a sleep that was refreshingly dreamless, though it lasted but a few moments: the shadow on the sundial registered no visible change when I opened my eyes. I remained where I was, quietly enjoying the sunshine, the scroll unread in my lap. When Brytha appeared and informed me that Scamander was at the dock, I was amazed that the time had passed so quickly. I rose regretfully and followed her, reminding her to wrap the scrolls with care. I would take them with me, I said (an arrangement Eutarchus has thoughtfully procured permission for). I shall spend tomorrow in dutiful study to make up for this afternoon's sloth.

Whatever this medicine is, I confess it seems to be working. The journey was the first pleasure I have experienced in months.

June 16

The past few days have been too crowded to find time for writing. The accounts had to be gone over, and Drusus was very trying until Camillus came. (He seems a pleasing young man, and very knowledgeable). Then there was the dinner party, and on the following day I ventured into town to do the marketing myself instead of sending Felix. In between these and other duties I have been faithfully reading Lucretius.

Propertius arranged the banquet without telling me, as a surprise, informing me only an hour before the guests came and bringing me a decanter of wine to accompany the news. It would be a small gathering, he assured me, of only our closest friends, who would be overjoyed to see that I was well again and receiving company. "I was afraid if I told you too far in advance you would take fright and refuse," he said. "Forgive me if I have erred, but I think it is time you resume relations with society." He then quoted Seneca, as is his wont, to the effect that the soul did violence to itself in turning its face away from those of its kind. He patted my hand, urging the wine to calm my nervousness. Eutarchus has put him up to this, I thought, which I found curiously reassuring: if the evening was part of my therapy, I had no choice but to participate. I relaxed, and was able to greet my guests calmly.

My fears proved groundless. The gathering included, aside from Drusus, Propertius and myself, Lucilla and Flavius, Camillus (the new tutor), Lucius Viranius, a professor of rhetoric at the collegiate, and, finally, best of all, Marcus and Aemilia, who have recently returned from Rome. I hadn't seen them in months and had missed Aemilia particularly, although I did not realize this until I saw her.

The conversation turned as usual to what was going on in the capital. From this it was but a step to the ritual laments for the decadence of the times and the sad state to which virtue has fallen under the emperors. Such talk, if repeated too often, can be a great bore, in addition to being depressing. Fortunately the discourse took a more original turn. It appears that there is a new history in circulation that traces in some detail the reigns of Augustus and Tiberius, and even of Nero. It is rumored that the author plans to continue it through the period of the recent civil war and into the reign of Vespasian himself. Naturally Rome is agog, for there are many still living who played a significant part in the events described.

According to Lucius, who introduced the topic, the author of the work is a daring, original young scholar by the name of Tacitus. Lucius has been fortunate enough to obtain a copy of the first volumes and is having them reproduced. He offered them as proof that our times are not as desperate as they seem, arguing that if such an unvarnished account of recent, even contemporary events could be openly published without fear of reprisal, then the precious heritage of freedom handed down to us by our ancestors could be considered still intact, even if we were no longer in form a Republic. If such truths were allowed free circulation among Roman citizens, he said, surely there was hope for an end to the gross abuses of power and debased practices that presently plagued us.

Here I thought I saw Camillus smile wryly to himself, but when he saw me looking at him he resumed a neutral expression and glanced away.

"It can be argued against me, of course, that I am too optimistic," Lucius went on, perhaps having registered Camillus' smile. "I am not gifted with the power of foreseeing the future, and I do not claim that works of art are the sole determinants of public morals, but I can't help believing that to commune with a mind such as this must itself be a stimulus to virtue. The prose, gentlemen, the exquisite prose!" And waving his goblet in the air, he ranted on—speaking quite well, actually, if a bit absurdly of the "lucidity" and "perfection of tone" achieved in this new work. Marcus, too, it turned out, had read the first volumes, and joined in singing the author's praise. I confess I was intrigued, and secured Lucius' promise to let Felix copy the scrolls when they are completed.

I noticed Camillus glance at me in some surprise when I said this, but whether because he thought I intended to ask him to perform such a task as part of his employment, or because he found it unusual that a slave like Felix should be literate I do not know.

As the conversation resumed, I was struck by the portrait of Livia that emerged. I gather that this new historian sees our esteemed first Empress as a profoundly reactionary influence on Augustus, whose sole fault, he claims, was his continual deference to her. It was she who counselled him on key appointments, she who ordained whether legions should be stationed in Syria and the boundaries of empire extended. In public she was the Mother of the Country, chaste, gracious, always shown in processions accompanied by a train of female children, but behind the scenes, according to this new history, she was a master of poison. She held public morality campaigns, inveighing against addiction to drink and the too frequent practice of abortion, but in private freely supplied the Emperor with prostitutes. It is Livia, it is asserted, who established the imperial succession; by the time of her death all hope that Rome might return to a Republic was extinquished. It was her policy of "subsidies and circuses" that held the masses in delusion, that and the trumpery religion she fostered; her arch-conservative beliefs that turned Augustus from a decent man willing to rule within the law to the tyrant he in the end became. Coming from great wealth and such an illustrious family, how could she have been expected to have any sympathy for the plight of the average citizen? And thus the harmony between the classes that had existed during the Republic was shattered . . . .

And so on. It never ceases to amaze me how all the ills of the world are attributed to the influence of women! Granted Livia possessed immense power, and used it to put into place a system of order these men dislike (which I too dislike, I hasten to add), but Augustus could have silenced her any time he chose. Why is he then not condemned? Remarkable as it is for an historian of our times to be censuring any of the royal family, this vaunted boldness of Tacitus seems to turn quite limp when it comes to the "divine" Augustus.

In any case, the chance for renewing the Republic was lost not in the reign of Augustus but during the reign of Caligula, when the Senate proved once and for all that it would not stand up to even the most outrageous abuses of power.

I grant that Livia was ruthless, deceitful, almost wholly without redeeming virtue, but perverse as it may be, there is a part of me that admires her. There is evidence in her of a ruined greatness, a rare combination of sharp intelligence and firmness of will. That she used her talents for devious ends is perhaps because as a woman she had to operate continually behind the scenes. It is men, after all, who rule this world, whether it be empire or Republic, yet every age blames its Tiberius on Agrippina, its Nero on Poppaea. Now they are making Livia out to be the Whore of Empire, blackening her image beyond recognition. Soon they will begin removing her statues and withdrawing from circulation the coins bearing her likeness.

These differing versions of history we are given (for the historical accounts we received in school concerning Augustus' and Livia's reign are very different from what this new historian is apparently saying) cannot help but call into question the validity of anyone's claims to truth, be he historian, philosopher, or natural scientist.

22

Which brings me to the scrolls I borrowed from Pomponius' library, which I have almost finished.

I find Lucretius, for the most part, tedious, no less so now than when I read him years ago at the collegiate. His main concern seems to be to console people about fears relating to the nature of life after death, as if the only reason people feared death was because they were afraid of imagined torments to come. This is not so in my case. I do not fear death because I fear an after-life: I know perfectly well there is nothing after dissolution. I do not so much fear the idea as detest it. I am outraged by it: it makes nonsense of everything, nullifies every act. What is all this toil and sacrifice and self-denial *for* if it does not matter how long or how brief one's stay on earth is? What is the point of "living for others" and offering one's self as a model of duty as we are continually exhorted to do if life on this earth is a pointless accident, as Lucretius assures us it is, and might just as well not have happened? What earthly good is virtue, even if it did accomplish its unlikely task of "raising the spiritual level of mankind"?

He keeps trying to persuade me that death is perfectly acceptable, perfectly "within the nature of things." It is an idea to which reason assents but from which the soul revolts. I cannot accept it. I do not.

June 17

I had my first private encounter with Camillus today, which took place in the courtyard by the pool. I was sitting there sewing when I glanced up and saw him coming and was struck again by how handsome he is. He is of medium height, with dark curls cropped close to his face. His features are finely modelled, his eyes candid and intelligent. Despite his reserve, there is a lovely springiness to his walk. He seems very young, although Propertius told

23

me earlier he is thirty-two: only five years younger than I. I was embarrassed by my consciousness of his physical presence, by the desire to exclaim aloud in wonder and delight, as one does upon discovering a newly opened flower. Fortunately I restrained such indecorous an impulse and inquired instead of his background.

He is a foundling who knows nothing of his blood relations. He was discovered as an infant at the base of the Columna Lactaria, where poor mothers abandon their children in the hope they will be taken into a childless home. Camillus, no doubt because he was an appealing child, was among the fortunate, adopted by a wealthy Syrian merchant living in Rome who practices the Hebrew faith. The boy was raised as a Roman, however, and sent to the best academies. After completing his studies there, he travelled to Athens and Alexandria where he stayed for several years, availing himself of their libraries. Since then he has made his living as a rhetorician and tutor.

When I inquired how Propertius had learned of him, he told me that his adopted mother, who is Roman, knows Eutarchus, who mentioned to her that we were looking for someone to take over Drusus' education. For his part Camillus had heard of Propertius' work in the theatre and longed to live again by the sea, which he had grown to love, he said, in Alexandria. He also felt a kinship with the landscape of the Campania, having made several visits here with his adopted father when he was a child. For these reasons he had accepted my husband's offer. He added that our home was everything he could wish, and that he was becoming very fond of Drusus, "your quick-minded, charming son," as he called him.

He offered to consult with me in detail about Drusus' proposed curriculum. I asked if it would deviate from what was normal for boys my son's age, and when he assured me it would not, I told him I would leave him free to proceed as he chose. I was being very formal: I wonder now if I sounded cold. The truth is I do not want to be involved with Drusus' education—Camillus is here in order to free me of that.

He bowed but looked faintly surprised. I assured him that I wanted, of course, to be kept informed of my son's progress. "We will meet from time to time," I said lightly, "here, in the afternoons, shall we?"

He agreed readily, as if the request was nothing unusual. Perhaps it was not, perhaps I felt myself colouring after hearing my words because only I and not he was aware that they could be misconstrued, that some might interpret what I had said as an invitation to flirtation. Immediately I asked myself if this is what I intended, and the stirring of desire I felt in response at the base of my stomach shocked me. I rose quickly, not knowing how much I was unwittingly communicating, and made hasty excuses to leave. I am afraid my tone as I dismissed him was barely gracious. Back in my room I found myself trembling.

I tremble now, thinking of it: with shame or anticipation, anxiety or joy? In some part the latter. I can hear a small voice crowing inside, saying "see, you are not as dead as you thought, you can still be aroused to desire." But the idea is alarming, and a worse one intrudes: that perhaps Propertius has hired this man deliberately to tempt me, even that he is granting me permission in advance to take Camillus as a lover if I choose. As if this lovely creature is his offering, his way of atoning for his impotence.

More outrageous still: it occurs to me that if it was Propertius who made the immediate decision, it was Eutarchus who devised the plan. Perhaps Camillus is meant to be a part of my cure, a tonic for my fears and depression.

Is there truth in any of these conceptions, or are such thoughts symptomatic of my illness?

Poor Camillus, to be the focus of them! What makes me think he would have the slightest inclination to become my lover even if Propertius has taken leave of his ethics and Eutarchus become a procurer, none of which I for a moment believe.

It must be illness. In future I must keep our intercourse as formal as possible, and set a more watchful eye on my tongue.

June 18

I was awakened in the middle of the night by another terrible dream. For an instant I felt it so clearly I thought it was still going on, even though my eyes were open.

I was in the Forum. People were walking about, vendors were hawking their products, children were playing on the steps of the Temple. Everything was as usual, but I was possessed with the sense that something strange was going on that I could not explain. Then I became aware that all the activity of the street was proceeding in silence. It was as if I had suddenly gone deaf. I glanced uneasily over my shoulder and was immediately struck with horror. There was a vast wall of mud moving toward me, sweeping everything in its path. It was still some distance away, but it was proceeding with shocking speed. It grew higher and higher, swelling into a monstrous wave. When it was almost upon me I saw that there were corpses in it, the arms and legs and torsos of people who had been swallowed up. I tried to scream, but no sound came from my mouth. I screamed again, soundlessly, and awakened.

For hours afterward I was afraid to return to bed. What causes such nightmares, what do they signify? Are they distorted descriptions of the present or portents of things to come? Shaking, I rose from the couch

and called Scribonia, telling her to fetch a lamp and my
scrolls, and for several hours I diligently copied long
passages from Lucretius until the images of the dream had
been extinguished and nothing but weariness remained.
Shortly before dawn I slept, but uneasily. The whole day
has been coloured with the grayness of fatigue. I feel
shrunken and diminished by dread, and am unable to
shake off a sense of foreboding.

It occurs to me that perhaps the dream presaged
only that—that the day was to be filled with thoughts and
images of death. It is possible that dreams are our bodies'
speech, that they are warnings that a low state of health is
approaching, a message delivered in exaggerated tongue.
It would be a relief to think so.

Surely it is no coincidence that this dream follows
my venturing into town the other day, something I hadn't
done for months. To my surprise I felt no anxiety. I
enjoyed the shops, the faces; I was even amused by the
graffiti on the walls (there is a municipal election next
week) instead of finding them repellent. The afternoon
was entirely pleasant, marred only by a disagreeable man
who served me rather rudely when I stopped for some
refreshment at the inn. It is as if the anxiety I expected to
experience and thought I had escaped returned to haunt
me in the dream. Is that possible?

June 23

It turned out to be a prediction of illness. I was in bed for
three days with fever and exhaustion and a painfully
swollen throat. Eutarchus was summoned and prescribed
poultices and herbs. On the fourth day I was still not fully
recovered, but it was Maternalia, a day honoring mother-
hood, and I knew I should get up.

I received from Propertius a lovely signet ring,

from Lucilla a serpentine bracelet, from Drusus a quaintly illustrated set of scrolls containing selections from Ovid. The latter I treasure: it was an unexpected gift, the only one that seemed genuinely from the heart. The poor child was terribly anxious as he presented it to me. I kissed him on the brow and soothed him, saying how enormously pleased I was, which made him blush. Camillus was with us, and like a fool I turned the conversation to him rather than Drusus, and before I was aware of it Drusus had slipped off. I did not see him again until dinner, and then he was withdrawn and quiet, so much so I grew anxious again about his health. He ate little, picking at his food. But that is the way he usually behaves when his sister is around, and Lucilla and Flavius were there, of course, inescapably.

What a lot of empty noise Lucilla makes! Mostly gossip, and protestations of how busy she is. She had to spend hours this week training her new hairdresser to do her hair in the intricate styles she affects (she refuses to look the same two days running). In addition, she said, she had had several appointments with her broker. Her what? I asked. It turns out she was talking about the man who advises her whether the income from Flavius' property would be better invested in jewels or in more land.

I was startled that Flavius would allow himself to be advised on such matters by someone as young as Lucilla. She is shrewd when it comes to finances, however, and willingly spends hours figuring out economies and pondering "investment decisions," as she calls them. Thank god Propertius always handles things of this sort for me; I manage our household budget from the money he gives me, but what we do with our surplus, if there is any, I don't concern my head about.

Flavius is looking well. Each time we see him I am more pleased than ever with our choice of son-in-law, but I feel uncomfortable around him because of my feeling that he deserves a better wife than my daughter. It is possible that with the years Lucilla will outgrow her vanity, but between now and then will be difficult for all concerned. Flavius seems much in love with her, however, and behaves with unfailing considerateness.

There is a fifteen-year difference in their ages, as there is between Propertius and myself, but there seems to me a far greater difference in maturity between them than I remember being true of the early years of our marriage, even though Lucilla had passed her eighteenth name day at the time of her wedding and I was barely sixteen at mine.

If he is tender and considerate of her, she is careless of him, deferring to him in nothing. I find her pertness objectionable, but Flavius treats it as harmless good spirits. He was even tolerant of her tipsiness when she drank three glasses of wine tonight, a quantity which borders on excess. I confess I was glad when the meal was over and I could plead weakness as an excuse for them to leave.

In truth, I was embarrassed to have my daughter's vulgarity exposed before Camillus. I was watching him throughout the evening, and though he was amiable and courteous, I could see he was under no illusions about her. He did not respond to her flirtatiousness but lightly brushed her sallies aside, refusing to be drawn in. I was struck by the way he continually included Drusus in the conversation whenever there was an opportunity. How kind he is to the child, and how pleased Drusus is with the attention! My heart went out to him.

As it did also to Propertius, who was trying his best to conceal his low spirits and ensure that I had a pleasant evening. Afterwards, when we talked, I learned that his petition to the magistrate to produce *Phaedra*, even in translation, has again been turned down.

When we came here it was because Propertius believed he would be allowed more opportunity to stage the classics than he had in Rome. He believes passionately

29

in the great works of the Greek tragedians, which are to him almost a religion. He believes in theatre as the conscience of the empire, a force that unites and elevates the citizenry, preventing their fragmentation into warring egos. I sometimes think Propertius longs for a return of the Republic and loathes imperial rule largely becasue it practices artistic censorship and panders to the worst instincts of the populace. All the city fathers will allow now are productions of ballet and mime; there is scarcely any real theatre left. The official reason for this is that the population has become so polyglot. Because of the continual influx of "foreigners" (their name for the slaves acquired through our conquests) those who speak the Roman tongue are in a minority. But the real reason for the present low state of the theatre is the Games. Once they reopened, serious drama no longer commanded an audience. To draw enough people to make it pay one must show works devoid of nuance or subtlety.

The irony is that we came to this city because Propertius believed it was one of the few places where serious theatre could still command a following. Years ago, in Nero's time, the Games were forbidden here, as punishment for a riot during a gladitorial contest in which several visiting dignitaries from Parthia were injured. Lacking other diversions, people flocked to the theatre, so much so an additional one was built. Propertius was able to work with the architect on its design, with the result that the facilities are everything he could wish; but the conditions which promised such rich opportunity at the start no longer exist. No sooner was the theatre completed than Vespasian lifted the imperial ban and the Games were reopened. In consequence the theatre has been degraded.

Because of this Propertius suffers, but nobly, without complaint. He reminded me the other day that bad as things are, they were infinitely worse in Rome in his father's time. The horrible spectacles directors were compelled to put on by Caligula make one shudder to recall, "dramas" in which Orestes was literally torn apart by lions or Medea burned alive in a real sheet of flame. The actors who suffered such treatment were condemned criminals, of course, not professionals, but the moral degradation to the director in having to comply with such orders was intolerable. There is nothing so terrible now, but still the vulgar farces Propertius is forced to produce, many of them little more than pornography, shame him. He is allowed to put on one worthwhile work for every three "popular" ones, and even then only if he can convince the city fathers that it will turn a profit.

I think I would feel more sympathy with him if he were honest about his feelings, if he would just once express anger or bitterness instead of forever maintaining that patient, imperturbable mask of his. I know before he speaks that he will utter some aphorism or other, some jewel about the wisdom of bowing before fate and accepting what the gods choose to give us. It irritates me.

He does not complain, but neither does he exhibit any pleasure. With me he is courteous and solicitous, with the children forbearing and kind.

I dislike myself for being irritated with him and avoiding him as I do; for all his faults he is an admirable man. There are times when out of gratitude for his kindness it occurs to me to visit his bed, but I shrink from the idea of his touch. Fortunately he seems to understand this and does not put himself forward.

I find my thoughts, when I am idle, increasingly circling around Camillus. I see his face long after he has left my actual vision, and sometimes imagine what it must feel like to inhabit his body. I follow him in my mind, when he walks down to the Bay in the evenings. Scribonia told me he does this. She said she saw him standing on the quay several times when she was digging for shellfish on the shore. He was watching the setting sun, she said,

31

standing far out on the stones, quite motionless. "A serious young man, isn't he, miss" she commented, "always thinking." It is true. I long to know his thoughts.

June 24

I will be making my second visit to Stabiae in a few days to obtain the remaining scrolls of *De Rerum Naturae*. I am determined to complete the work, but with diminished expectations that it holds for me any key. What began so promisingly has so far turned out to be a disappointment. "We must grasp well," he says, "the principle by which the courses of the sun and moon go on and the force by which everything on earth proceeds, but above all we must find out by keen reason what the soul and the nature of the mind consist of, and what thing it is which frightens our minds if we are under the influence of disease; meets and frightens us too when we are buried in sleep. This terror and darkness of mind we propose to dispell by an understanding of the aspect and law of nature . . . ."

Such passages piqued my curiosity, but although Lucretius does indeed explain the workings of the forces of nature with "keen reason" (and with more copious examples than I would have wished), I do not see that he has contrived to explain, as he promises, "what the soul and the nature of the mind consist of, and what frightens us when we are buried in sleep."

My criticisms may be hasty; perhaps these subjects are dealt with toward the end. However, he seems to me remarkably adept at raising questions he does not answer and pretending to triumphs not fairly won. He seems to believe, for example, that by banishing all belief in the gods he will banish fear; as if by proving to us that the soul is mortal and that it perishes utterly with the body's demise we shall achieve peace of mind. Everything dies, he repeats: "The walls too of the great world itself shall be stormed and fall to decay and crumbling ruin."

I gather this message is supposed to afford me relief, as if my problem is that I believe that this mad world is run by gods! In fact it is the opposite: I see little purpose in living *because* I can discern no visible gods directing history, *because* there seems no design or plan or rhyme or reason to the fate meted out to human beings. Or to the poor animals, for that matter: Drusus' favorite cat has developed stones and must be put to sleep. It cries out in pain every time it urinates; Drusus is terribly upset about it.

Still, there are snippets here and there in the work which are stimulating. For example, Lucretius insists that mind and body are inseparable, saying "It is plain that the faculty of the body and the faculty of the mind cannot feel separately, each alone without the other's power; sense is kindled throughout our flesh and blown into flame between the two by joint motions on the part of both . . . ."

"Sense . . . blown into flame . . . by joint motions" of flesh and soul. When I read that, I could not help seeing, in my mind, Camillus. But what doesn't make me think of him lately? The fact that he is so much on my consciousness is disquieting.

Does not the act of relating these feelings exaggerate them? Would it not be better to be silent? Eutarchus' counsel was to write of whatever possessed me, but I fear the process not only fails to exorcize the posession but deepens it. I do not know: I cannot judge, any more than I can judge what happened this afternoon.

He joined me as I was walking in the garden, ostensibly to report on Drusus' progress. After he finished his report (a catalogue of praise, for the most part), he lingered. I sensed that he wished to say something further but wasn't sure how to begin. When I probed, he spoke hesitantly of the growing physical affection between himself and my son. The child had several times put his arms around him, he said, adding that he had not discouraged the embrace. He wanted to know if I thought in future he should forego such gestures. "The relations between Drusus and myself are innocent," he explained, "but I am concerned lest the appearance seem otherwise. Forgive me for saying so, but the child is in need of affection. He is at a difficult age, one that poses problems even for those untroubled by illness. He is approaching his fourteenth nameday, is he not?"

"In September," I answered. "We are already making plans for the ceremony."

He nodded. "He is looking forward to it, I know; he has mentioned it several times. Yet I suspect it also makes him fearful." He glanced away, as if debating whether to go further. He is very endearing when he is earnest like this; I am unused to earnestness combined with grave. "All of us at that age long to become men and imitate the dignity we think belongs to manhood," he resumed, "but at the same time there is a part of us that wants to remain a child, as if we know intuitively that that is where freedom lies. It is an age that looks both ways at once; Drusus longs for maturity but fears it also, fearing he may not come up to the mark."

I assured him that I had no objection to his responding to Drusus' embraces and that it was good of him to express concern. I tried to say this easily, but I am afraid I made a poor disguise of my feelings. The phrase, "the child is in need of affection," had sunk into my heart like a stone. What kind of woman, I thought, hired a stranger to give her son the love he needs?

Camillus must have sensed something of what I was feeling, for he surprised me by making an unexpected proposal. He has continued Drusus' Latin lessons, which involve the declamation of verse. "Your son has an excellent ear for prosody," he said, "but he seems to prefer your

34

reading to mine. He claims, not without justice I am sure, that your voice is more musical. I wonder if you would consider resuming one weekly reading with him. I am sure he misses you and that the improvement in his health would be marked if he saw you privately on a more regular basis." He paused, giving me time to consider before adding, "Forgive me if I am intruding beyond my station, but I thought I would ask this of you in the confidence that if I am being indiscreet you will not hesitate to tell me."

I flushed and looked away, wondering if he was oblivious to the ambiguity of his request. Wasn't it, beneath the surface, a test to determine what degree of informality between us was allowed? His remark was more than "indiscreet." What he had said could be construed by some as a piece of insolence, a reproof of my coldness as a mother. I knew he was aware of the risk he was taking, and I was impressed by the courage that gave him voice. Impressed also by his diplomacy—for the reproof, if such it was, was offered with great gentleness.

Thinking about it now I see the indiscretion not in the request itself, but in something more complex. It is not the prospect of a deepened involvement with Drusus that alarms me (although that presents problems of its own) as the greater degree of intimacy with Camillus the project will entail. We will be seeing each other with greater frequency. Is it possible he is unaware of the agitation his physical presence causes me?

I was inwardly thrown into confusion, but I promised to do what he asked and suggested Thursday afternoons. When I inquired if I should continue with Vergil, he ventured that something lighter might be more appropriate, so the occasion would be "wholly in the category of pleasure." We agreed I would let Drusus make the choice, after which he bowed and took his leave.

His proposal was well intended, and I am grateful to him for having made it, whatever the complications.

Instead of seeing his gesture as impertinence or unconscious seduction, I can equally see it, if I choose, as simply an attempt to assure me that he doesn't want to replace me in Drusus' affections. Or even more, as an attempt at healing—not only of Drusus, but of me, as if he knows my grief at the separation between us and is offering this as a cure.

What is it about this man that so attracts me? I tell myself it is only his beauty that stirs me, but it is something more. He calls to something deeper, something which frightens me. My resolutions to put him from consciousness are turning out to be worthless: I look forward with impatience to future meetings.

June 25

I seem to have become abnormally concerned about my appearance in the past few days. Is the return of vanity a sign of health or further evidence of morbidity? Whenever I catch sight of myself in the mirror I am shocked.... A thin worn face looks back at me, the skin showing signs of aging. When I am depressed this does not concern me; I rarely see myself then, or if I do the figure in the glass appears remote and umimportant. Now that I am getting better (if that is what is happening) I find myself wondering whether I shouldn't buy some of those concoctions they sell in the salons at the baths, mixtures of honey and asses' milk which derive, according to the vendors, from Poppaea's secret recipes.

I ordinarily consider such concerns contemptible, manifestations of unwholesome vanity, but now I keep thinking I should do something with myself, perhaps have my hair done in a more becoming fashion. The woman who looks back at me in the mirror seems frighteningly lifeless.

June 27

At Stabiae yesterday, Brytha met me at the entrance, saying her mistress wished to see me. I was taken aback by the news. Her mistress—was Pomponius' wife here then? I immediately grew anxious, not having anticipated any encounter with the owners of this villa. I was led to a side patio, where a beautiful woman in a pale yellow robe was reclining on a couch. She rose as I approached and graciously extended her hand. "I am Clio," she said in a voice as harmonious as her features. "We am most honored to receive your visits and welcome you to our dwelling. I have heard much of your husband, of whom Pomponius speaks always with praise."

I seated myself across from her and tried not to stare. No wonder she can afford to have someone as pretty as Brytha around: she is probably the loveliest woman I have ever seen—tall and graceful, with thick black hair, smooth olive skin and clear, wide-spaced green eyes. Her movements are those of a dancer, her bearing and expression self-assured, almost regal.

She seemed also highly intelligent. She drew me out skillfully, saying she was delighted to hear of my studies and that someone was making use of the library in their absence. She asked with what works I had begun, and when I told her she smiled in amusement. "Eutarchus has planned for you a diet of the Stoics, I see," she said, as if she didn't altogether approve. "Still," she added, "some have derived nourishment from such works, and I suppose they are as good a place as any to start. If they should prove indigestible I am sure you will go on to something else, yes? and if that happens, I hope you will allow me to make alternative suggestions; I know our holdings well."

I assured her that I would be happy to receive her advice at any time and the conversation turned to what was going on in Rome. The current scandal is that Julia Berenice has come back to the capital. Vespasian exiled her to Judaea four years ago, but now that he is in weakened health she has been bold enough to return and openly resume her affair with Titus. It is even rumored that he plans to marry her, despite the fact that she is a Jewess and twenty-eight years older than he. It is feared that Vespasian's anxiety over his heir may shorten his life.

I asked if the senators and rhetoricians were denouncing Julia Berenice in the public forums and again stirring up rancour as they did four years ago. Oddly enough, public denunciation is apparently muted this time. I suggested that perhaps everyone sensed that power was passing from Vespasian to Titus and that no one wished prematurely to try his temper.

"Perhaps," Clio answered, "but I should also consider the possibility that prejudice against women in high places has softened. She really is an extraordinary woman, you know; I knew her briefly when she was last in Rome. Enormously wealthy, of course, and beautiful even at fifty-one, but brilliant as well. Why else do you think Titus would be so besotted with her, unless she is a sorceress. Clearly she possesses a power of some sort."

The same sort of power Clio herself has, I thought, for by then I was fairly in awe of her. She spoke smoothly, as if she was only saying the obvious, but there was a hint of mystery in her words, a suggestion of worlds I knew nothing of, and I do not mean alone the world of the upper reaches of the court. I had expected her to take the general tone about Julia, whose reputation is that of a foreign adventuress of the worst sort, not come to her defense.

"Perhaps the prejudice against Jews has softened then as well," I ventured, at which Clio laughed, as if I had spoken in irony. "You are right, I am being sentimental," she said. "Julia will no doubt lose her struggle and end up in exile, permanently this time. Weakened Vespasian may be, but he is far from being powerless, and there are more people than Vespasian who are opposed to Julia

Berenice and everything she stands for."

I wondered what she meant by that but felt it would be an intrusion to ask.

She is obviously a well-educated woman. She is from Athens, she told me, but didn't mention her family or how she and Pomponius came to be betrothed. She will be here irregularly throughout the summer; I gather she finds Rome overly stimulating and feels the need to escape from it now and then. She expressed the hope that we would occasionally meet, and I took this as my cue to leave her. I think she wanted to assure me that my privacy in future visits would not be disturbed.

I took my way to the library and spent the remainder of the afternoon on Lucretius, resisting the temptation to wander out to the garden. I managed to get through the whole of Book IV, which I had never read before. It deals primarily with the senses and contains some curious items. For example, Lucretius claims that man's belief in the gods originated in dreams. Finding nothing in the real world that was immune to suffering and death, man dreamed of idealized figures. "In sleep he saw these creatures perform miracles yet saw on their part no fatigue from the effort." Thus he attributed to them supernatural powers. We create gods, he says, out of ignorance of the way the forces of nature operate; then we bow down to them in superstitious terror and propitiate their imagined displeasure and wrath.

His irreverence amused me, as did the things he had to say about sexual love. I have been told that the followers of Epicurus, among whom Lucretius is considered one of the more prominent, hold fleshly pleasures to be among the highest good. If so, Lucretius is no Epicurean. I was surprised to find him treating the pleasure of love quite negatively, referring to it most often as a snare, an inducement to folly and unnecessary pain. He admits the power of Venus and freely acknowledges that it is in the nature of things for male to seek female; he is even modern enough to hold that the female also seeks and derives pleasure from congress ("Again and again, I repeat, pleasure is common to both participants"), but he counsels us to flee the approach of passion and to be on guard beforehand so as not to be drawn in. "To avoid falling into the toils of love is not so hard as, after you are caught, to get out of the nets you are in and to break through the meshes of Venus."

Odd that he should cast Venus in the guise of huntress, ensnaring her victims with love as the net. He seems to have confused her with Diana. Why does he see love in such a fearful light? What is it that men fear so?

He is also eccentric in other ways. I was rather offended by the passage where he presumes to tell the female that she should make no movements during the love act. Such movements "hinder and stand in the woman's way of conceiving," he states, "for she drives the furrow out of the direct path of the share and turns away from the proper spots the stroke of the seed." He adds that only harlots move their bodies in rhythm with the man, and that their purpose is to avoid conception as well as to stimulate their partner. Idiot man. As if our bodies' movements do not concern our own pleasure and have nothing to do with the prospect of a child. In any case there are far more effective methods of preventing conception than that.

All told, the work seems a strange mixture of folly and wisdom. I shall be glad to be done with it.

There was a partial eclipse of the sun yesterday. I was out in the courtyard cutting flowers and felt the sky darken. Would I have been more frightened if I had been totally ignorant of the nature of the forces that were operating, if I had not been influenced by Lucretius' attitude, in fact? The slaves were very upset by the occurrence; I found Scribonia shrunk into a corner with her eyes staring from her head. It took me some time to calm her.

What I experienced was not so much fright as disorientation, and for this Lucretius' explanations offer no remedy. I grant that the phenomenon of an eclipse is regular and ordered, that it is repeated in time and passes with time, that it does not herald any cataclysm or give us in reason any evidence for fearing that the sun's light could suddenly be extinguished. The problem is that our minds are so constructed that we cannot help thinking "what if?" No matter how strenuously we cling to reason, the question "what if" cannot be permanently banished. We cannot always prevent ourselves from thinking "But what if the sun *should* go out some day," whereupon we shiver, for our bodies repond to what we conceive in our imaginations as well as what we feel on our skin. Unfortunately, I can conceive only too vividly a world of total destruction; it is the landscape of my dreams.

It is to wean myself from the habit of the imagination that I am engaging in this course of study. Yet something in me resists, as if I am not sure whether the cure is preferable to the disease.

July 1

I have not had occasion to see Camillus alone in the past few days, but I did have a warm conversation with Drusus. He is looking much better, not nearly as pale as a month ago. He seems to be putting on weight; his face looks slightly fuller.

We embraced, and I asked how he was progressing in his studies. "Camillus is teaching me many exciting things," he said enthusiastically. "Did he tell you about my declamation yesterday? The topic he set was 'Resolved: that Rome should adhere to its present boundaries and make no further territorial conquests.' I was to pretend that I was Brutus before the Civil War, delivering a speech in the Senate. It took me hours and hours to compose it, but it was very good, I think. At least Camillus said it was."

"I'm sure it was, Drusus," I replied. "But what an unusual topic: why did Camillus choose Brutus as the speaker?"

"Brutus was a Republican, mother," he said patiently. "It was Caesar's wars of conquest that destroyed the Republic."

I looked at him in amusement. "The army grew too powerful," he continued, speaking as if he had been coached. "It was they who put Julius Caesar in power and have determined all the emperors since. In addition, with so many conquered peoples from the wars, the price of slaves dropped so they were cheap enough to be used to work the land. This drove the small farmers into bankruptcy, and instead of being a society of equal, independent men we became a society of rich and poor, with a small number of rich landowners and an enormous number of slaves. Under such conditions there could be no Republic."

I was amused at his seriousness but remonstrated with him, pointing out that the majority of the population were freedmen, who were neither rich nor slaves.

"The majority are the poor, mother," came the quick retort, "and politically speaking they are no freer than slaves. Most are so poor their votes can be purchased by any Senator who wants them. That was what Julius Caesar did. He bribed his soldiers with 1,000 drachmas each; in addition, he bestowed gifts on thousands of other voters."

"All of this may be so," I said, not wishing to undermine Camillus' authority but at the same time startled at the unorthodox view of history he seemed to be teaching my son. "But do you not think such a speech as you put in Brutus' mouth would be considered unpatriotic, Drusus?

Rome's mastery of other lands has had positive results too, you know. Our 'conquests' as you call them have extended civilization to places which were purely barbaric before our soldiers came, places where people painted their faces blue and made human sacrifices. They lived rather wretchedly, you know. We have brought them law, art, roads, irrigation, education. Surely you agree that the people now within the empire are better off than they were before? Caesar's accomplishments shouldn't be dismissed so lightly."

"There is truth in what you say of course, mother, but what Camillus says seems also true," he replied with a frown. "In any case, *he* liked my declamation."

I hastened to tell him I was sure I would think highly of it also; then I proposed that we resume our reading aloud together once a week. I asked what he would like to work on, telling him he was free to choose. "Any poet, mother?" he asked, and when I nodded, promptly said "Ovid." Without thinking, I agreed.

"Do you mean it?" he persisted. "You have not asked which book."

"I assume you meant *The Metamorphoses,*" I said, but no, he told me, what he wanted to read was *The Art of Love.* I did not know whether to laugh or be shocked. I have never known Drusus to tease, but surely he could not be suggesting that I read aloud to him a manual on the art of seduction? I scolded him, reminding him that this work had been banned since Augustus' decree, whereupon he demanded to know why we had a copy if it was against the law. I explained that it wasn't against the law to possess the book if you had owned it before the decree, that it was his grandfather's copy, which Propertius had inherited. "In those times it was a sign that one believed in freedom of speech to possess it," I added. "It was a mark of being a Republican."

"Why can we not read it, then?" he asked with

feigned innocence. "We're Republicans, are we not?"

I told him that what was acceptable for an adult was not necessarily acceptable for a child and that I was surprised that he should even make the suggestion. He then wanted to know if we could read it when he was old enough, "when he was fourteen." I conceded the point but added that by then he would be old enough to read it privately, and before he could quibble further I told him it would have to be *The Metamorphoses* or nothing. "I shall use the copy you gave me, shall I," I coaxed, "the one with the lovely illustrations?"

This proposal mollified him (it was no doubt what he expected in the first place) and we agreed on the time: Thursdays, at mid day.

Thus Camillus' suggestion bears its first fruit.

July 2

Dinner last night with Aemilia and Marcus, who are leaving for Rome very soon. It was lovely to be in their home again. Aemelia has had the triclinium redone, with new murals of soft grays and violets that create a wonderfully soothing atmosphere. The evening could not have been improved upon, from the food, which was various and excellently prepared, to the music and conversation. How restful to be among people whose outlook on the world is so similar to one's own that you do not constantly have to be on guard against some unexpected dissonance! The four of us have known each other so long now we are fully aware of our differences (few as they are) and easily steer around them. The result is that the conversation flows smoothly, punctuated with intervals of silence in which we relax and absorb the sounds of the fountain.

Propertius opened the talk by inquiring about the theatre situation in Rome. From Marcus' report, it is even worse there than here. A recent performance of *Antigone* played to a half-empty house while people fought in the streets for admission to the chariot races. According to Aemelia, there are pictures of charioteers everywhere. The obsession with gambling, it seems, has become even more pronounced, and the Games themselves increasingly violent.

We discussed what this signified. Marcus claimed that all one heard in the baths, indeed in the lecture halls and forums as well, was arguments about the strengths and weaknesses of the currently favored gladiators and charioteers. The mania for gambling is ruining many families. Propertius saw this as further evidence of breakdown in the social order, which in turn was a consequence of the failure of either the official gods or the state to command the peoples' allegiance. Without faith virtue was undermined, he said, and materialism became the deadly substitute.

Marcus agreed, but suggested another reason: that there were too many religions available. "Why should anyone follow the prescriptions of any one faith," he asked, "when there are so many offering themselves as the sole guide to truth? All are discredited: religion has turned into a marketplace, with a variety of priests hawking their wares. The problem is the way the city has been flooded with foreigners. We cannot outlaw these people for we are dependent on their labor, and naturally they bring with them their gods, which it would be useless to forbid."

I was curious whether the foreigners were as attracted to the Games as the Romans were, and was told by Marcus that it was hard to judge, but that most of them seemed to be, except for the Jews, of course, who shun them absolutely. What then, I wondered, was the source of their popularity? Aemilia proposed that the obsession with gaming arose from the mindset that saw the world in terms of victory and defeat, which in turn was a sign of the

growth of the military's influence. The two most commonly heard justifications for the gladiatoral contests, she
argued, were that they served as a deterrent to crime (since
most of those killed are criminals), and that the courage
exhibited by the doomed men inspired the people to 'Spar-
tan virtue' by inuring them to the spectacle of pain. "But
why should this particular virtue be so esteemed?" she
asked. "It is only a virtue in time of war. If Rome did not
have such enormous armies we would not be constantly
extending our borders at the expense of other races; if we
practiced a policy of diplomacy, we would not need violent
sport to accustom us to the prospect of violent death."

Marcus admitted there was something in this but
added that he still favored Propertius' argument that the
increasing popularity of the Games had to do with the
collapse in a belief in divinity. "A society whose only challenge is the pursuit of material wealth offers to the spirit
nothing but a desert. The Games are a way of filling empty
lives, giving people a temporary sense of purpose, namely
'to win.' What it is that is being won, and whether the prize
is of any value, of course, is not considered. The spectator
lives only for 'victory' and the flush of power that comes
when his side achieves it. This is why violence in sport is
more marked now, I think, why the gladiatoral contests are
increasingly being fought to the death: for in addition to
the thrill of profit if you have placed your money on the
right man, there is also the heady sense of possessing the
power of life and death over the loser. With a gesture of
your wrist, a man either lives or dies."

"Ah, but isn't that heady sense you speak of also a
matter of the spectator feeling that he is somehow conquer-
ing death?" Aemilia asked. "The wild beast contests, for
example. What are they but the staging of a symbolic
drama in which man triumphs over that part of nature he
most fears? From the accounts I have heard (I confess I
have not witnessed such spectacles myself) they seem to

me similar in theme to many fine dramas in which civilization triumphs over brute evil."

Propertius, of course, demurred at this, objecting vigorously to any comparison between the theatre and the blood sports of the arena. Whatever such contests might symbolize, it was real flesh that was lacerated in the Games and real blood that was spilled. No breath of virtue could possibly be derived from carnage, he asserted. It was folly to say that watching such spectacles performed the cathartic function that Aristotle accorded tragic drama. The presentation of actual violence did not purge the aggressive emotions, as some professed, but exascerbated them: how else explain the enormous rise in violent crime reported throughout the empire, particularly in the capital, where it was not uncommon for people to be robbed and beaten even in broad daylight? He quoted Seneca's statement, 'I came home from the contests more greedy, more cruel and inhuman, because I had been among human beings.' "No," he said, shaking his head, "I am afraid our passion for games is yet another sign that our society is increasingly giving itself over to its worst instincts. We are living in decadent times. Piety is becoming a relic of the past, honour a vanishing shade."

He gave a melancholy sigh at this but then checked himself, adding dutifully that this was all the more reason why we should concern ourselves only with those things that lie within the compass of our wills and not bewail events over which we have no control.

When asked what I thought, I replied that I agreed with Aemilia, that surely Rome's history of conquest and the consequent growth of the military had something to do with the habit of mind that viewed the world in terms of victory and loss. "However," I added, "the empire has been at peace for more than a decade; the present borders seem firm. Perhaps the involvement with games can be considered a positive sign; perhaps it functions as a displacement of man's impulse to war."

I was going to elaborate but Marcus objected. "I wouldn't be so sure our present boundaries are fixed," he cautioned. "We know nothing of Titus yet except that he is an excellent general. If the Parthians continue to subvert our Armenian province there may well be war with Parthia. I am not at all sure we will be content to remain within our present limits; there is certainly no guarantee of it. As long as there is still a part of the world where our trade does not dominate our merchants will want it secured, and our generals will be only too happy to accommodate them. And it is they who legitimate our emperors, remember, if indeed they do not occupy the post themselves, as Titus soon will."

I was reminded of the declamation topic Camillus had set Drusus, which I would have brought up but for a reluctance to speak of it without having first mentioned it to Propertius.

"Not even Titus would think of taking on the Parthians," Propertius intervened. "He knows it would mean our mutual destruction. Rome is too weak internally for so major an adventure, our troops are spread too thin, which the generals know better than anyone. It is all we can do to find cohorts to handle the rebellions in the Germanic lands; to raise additional armies to fight and occupy Parthia is out of the question. Who would we use for soldiers—slaves? Mercenaries? Our wealth is not inexhaustible. The money the army spends right now threatens to bankrupt the treasury. No, I think Claudia is right, we have reached our limits and will not soon seek new territory. Of course," he added after a pause, "there is no accounting for madness in high places, and our Caesars, gods though they may be, have been known on occasion to depart from the rule of reason."

"Speaking of which," Aemelia said, "have you heard of the new edicts calling on women to bear more babies, Claudia? Even without war with Parthia, Rome needs soldiers. It is our civic duty to bear them, according to Vespasian, who is making loud exhortations to us to be more forthcoming. The Senate is considering outlawing abortion again. Furthermore, they are planning to shorten the time you are allowed to stay widowed or divorced from eighteen months to sixteen, with the penalty for choosing otherwise being the forfeiture of half your dowry. Really, what are we coming to?"

Dear Aemelia, I will miss her. She is a lively and comforting spirit, and we see them too little. They have invited us to visit them in Rome, of course, but I do not think I am yet up to such a journey. Perhaps later in the summer, if my spirits continue to improve.

I wonder if I should question Camillus about the history he is teaching my son. His views are clearly unorthodox but I am afraid he might interpret my questions as criticism, or worse, as attempted censorship. I do not want him to think me intolerant, but on the other hand I do not want Drusus growing up with dangerous views either. At least not before he has reached the age of judgement.

The child's loneliness bothers me. I wish Propertius would make more time for him. I see no reason why he could not take him to the theatre every now and then, now that his health is better. I will propose the idea—but why does he not think of things like this himself?

Odd. I see I have always taken for granted Propertius' formality with Drusus, as if this is the ideal way for fathers to relate to their sons. It is how my father treated me—he was unfailingly kind, but at the same time distant and preoccupied. Such behavior seems empty to me now, insufficient, as does the evenness of temper and tranquillity of mind which Propertius is so proud of. It strikes me as little more than a want of feeling, an abstractedness from the senses that I have come to distrust. What he said at dinner tonight, for example, was quite reasonable, but it was also windbaggery. No one could be more sincere, and yet he always seems to me slightly false.

Nevertheless, I shall put to him my proposal about Drusus. He will comply, I am sure, and apologize for not having thought of it himself. What have I to complain of, really, in such a husband? I am perverse.

The subject of the Games still piques my curiosity. Perhaps I should attend one; I haven't been to the arena in years. It occurs to me that the principal attraction of contests of any sort is that they offer a model of order and coherence. If the preoccupation with sport satisfies a longing in the human breast, it is perhaps not so much the desire to win that is operative as the desire to engage in something governed by clear rules. The charioteers steer a fixed course, the regulations of the race are undeviating. Perhaps it is life's uncontrollableness we unwittingly seek to master by means of this substitute activity. For the spectator, games present a wonderful simplification: in them the key elements are controlled, unlike our real lives with their messy irrelevancies and unexpected shocks, their sudden passions and undeserved pain.

Games "make sense": we attend them because we wish to delude ourselves that it is within our compass to triumph over chance and fate.

July 3

I had another inexplicable dream last night. In it I was playing backgammon with Drusus, who was winning until I threw three lucky turns in a row. He suddenly became angry and deliberately tipped the board over, scattering the pieces to the floor. I knelt to retrieve them, but when I straightened it was not Drusus opposite me but Lucilla, as if it had been she at the board all along. Like Drusus, she was furious. She began taking off her rings and flinging them at me, saying "I will not live with him, I will not, I don't care what you say." I was bewildered, not understanding who she was talking about. "Not live with your father?" I asked, but she ran out of the room without answering me. Then I saw Camillus through the window, walking in the garden. He felt my eyes on him and raised his head. I had the impression there was something he wanted to tell me, but before he could speak I awoke.

I remember writing yesterday that the attraction of games was that they presented a model of order and coherence, that in them events were controlled, not subject to unexpected blows or ungoverned passions. The dream rebukes me, turning the idea upside down, like Drusus flipping the board over.

Both my children lash out at me in the dream. They are angry, but why I do not understand. And why did Camillus look at me so mournfully? What was he trying to say?

I intended to go to Stabiae this morning, but a sudden storm prevented me. When the weather calmed in the afternoon I sent Felix to return the scrolls with a message asking to borrow the first volumes of the *Discourses of Epictetus*. Clio sent them back with him, together with a note expressing disappointment at not seeing me but wishing me well. She is returning to Rome for several weeks, so I shall not see her again soon.

To ward off my melancholy I have spent the evening with the work and find myself strangely attracted to it. His arguments are similar to Lucretius', but his tone is more appealing. It is more personal, more intimate; one comes to know the man more as a human being than an abstract voice. His language casts a special spell, rather like entering the cool stillness of the temple after the glare and clutter of the marketplace. I find my unruly questions left behind, slipped off with my sandals. . . .

I began with the essay, "On Things In Our Power

and Things Not In Our Power," which struck a responsive chord. His argument, if I follow it right, is this:

The one divine gift the gods bequeathed us is the faculty of reason, the self-reflective power that allows us to order and judge our impressions. In this area alone do we possess freedom. In all else—in what happens to our bodies, to our feelings when our loved ones are taken from us, the nature and manner of our deaths—we are determined, at the mercy of stimuli from within and without over which we have no control. Our reason, our will, is god-given, but it is enmeshed, through its links with the body, in the material world.

When Epictetus was asked by a student why the gods, in creating man, withheld from him complete freedom, he answered, "For my part I think that if they could have entrusted us with those other powers they would have done so, but they were quite unable to. Prisoners on the earth and in an earthly body and among earthly companions, how was it possible that we should not be hindered by external fetters?"

We are not, then, free to choose our fate, but we are free to choose what to make of it. It lies within our will to surmount our destiny by freely choosing our response. "I must die," says Epictetus, "but must I die groaning? I must be imprisoned, but must I whine as well? I must suffer exile. Can any one then hinder me from going with a smile, and with good courage, and at peace?"

He offers as a model of how one should confront one's fate the behavior of Agrippinus when he was informed that his trial was proceeding in the Senate. "Good luck to it," the noble Senator is said to have replied, "but the fifth hour is come" (this was the hour when he used to take exercise and have a cold bath). When later they came and told him he had been condemned, he asked whether to exile or death. "To exile," was the response. "And my property?" "It is not confiscated." "Well then, let us go and

52

dine."

"Here you see the result of training as training should be," Epictetus comments. "I must die, must I? If at once, then I am dying: if soon, I will dine now, as it is time for dinner, and afterwards when the time comes I will die. And die how? As befits one who gives back what is not his own." It was this last phrase that particularly struck me: the concept that our bodies, our lives, are on loan to us by nature, to whom we must return them with grace, is an unusual way to look at death, at least for me. It is one I find oddly appealing.

I am sure I don't really believe it—believe that ordinary people can continuously hold in mind so noble a conception, that is—but how beautiful to be reminded of models of Roman virtue, to know that some men, at least, are capable of transcending our common selfishness, even if the rest of us cannot. Men like Socrates and Epictetus seem genuinely to have conquered fear; and as for bitterness that life is short and can be arbitrarily cut off, they dismiss it as a childish complaint.

Epictetus claims that most of our unhappiness comes from mental error, that we all need training in correcting erroneous habits of mind. If this is true, it would seem wise to commit to memory certain of these new ways of thinking. So:

On suicide: "Men as you are, wait upon God. When he gives you the signal and releases you from this service, then you shall depart; but for the present be content to dwell in this country where He has appointed you to dwell."

I notice, however, that he qualifies this statement with the reminder that suicide is a legitimate course of action if life becomes unbearable, or honour threatened. "Remember that the door is always open. Do not be a greater coward than the children, but do as they do. Children, when things do not please them, say 'I will not play any more.' So, when things seem to you to reach that point, just say 'I will not play any more' and depart, instead of staying to moan."

On Education: "Education consists in learning to distinguish between things in our power and things not in our power. In our power are will and all operations of the will, and beyond our power are the body, the parts of the body, possessions, parents, brothers, children, country, in a word—those whose society we share."

"As we pity the blind and the lame, so should we pity those who are blinded and lamed in their most sovereign faculties—the reason and the moral sense."

"No man is master of another; our masters are only death and life, pleasure and pain."

The conclusion of the scroll filled me for an instant with joy. I do not share Epictetus' piety, but I could not help being touched as I read the following: "If I were a nightingale, I should sing as a nightingale, if a swan, as a swan, but as I am a rational creature I must praise God. This is my task and I will not abandon this duty, so long as it is given me. I invite you to join in the same song."

It is an appealing invitation. Alas, I cannot remember the tune.

July 5

When I joined Drusus this afternoon he was bubbling over with enthusiasm at the prospect of going with his father to the theatre Saturday. "Eutarchus says I am well enough, mother, may I go?" he asked.

Despite the fact that such an outing was my suggestion, I didn't entirely approve, for the play Propertius is presently rehearsing is one of Plautus' more ribald comedies. I reflected, however, that Drusus was no longer quite a child, and that some of what we were about to read in Ovid also contained highly questionable passages. Thinking it would be hypocritical to withhold my consent, I gave it. Perhaps I didn't wish to appear censorious around Camillus, who took his leave shortly after this although we urged him to stay. Clearly he wishes the time between Drusus and myself to be private.

"Where does he go when he is not with us, mother?" Drusus inquired when he was gone. "Why does he not sleep here?"

I had been unaware that such was the case. On questioning Drusus, I learned that he had gone to Camillus' bedchamber to ask him something one night after dinner and had been told by one of the slaves that Camillus spent most of his nights in town. "You must have noticed that he excuses himself early," Drusus said, and then startled me by asking with great seriousness, "Do you think he has a lover, mother?"

I had not considered it my business to know Camillus' whereabouts and had assumed he slept in the apartments we provided for him. As to his having a lover, I acknowledged with a pang that it was quite possible; no doubt many women were in love with so attractive a man.

"That is not the sort of thing one asks, Drusus," I said. "It is the essence of good manners to respect people's privacy. Camillus is a free man who may go where he likes; I hope you have not been impertinent enough to question him."

"I did," he confessed, hanging his head, "but he wouldn't tell me; he reproved me, like you did. Isn't he a wonderful person though, mother! I hope he finds a wife. I think he is lonely."

"I am sure he has many friends, Drusus," I said, "in addition to us. Why should he be lonely?"

"A man needs a woman, mother, you know that. Every man has a duty to have children."

I laughed. "Is that something Camillus taught

you?"

"Of course. What would become of Rome if her citizens all remained childless? It is our duty to the gods and the state to be unselfish. Everyone knows that."

So, I thought, amused, at least some of what he is teaching my son is orthodox.

I seated myself beside him and unrolled the first scroll of *The Metamorphoses*. We exclaimed over the illustrations for a while and then I began. It is a beautiful poem, really; I had forgotten how enchanting its language is. I have not read it since I was a girl (although no mother read it to me, I read it myself). I was struck by how similar the beginning is to Lucretius, though the theme is here treated lyrically rather than in the epic mode. Ovid traces the world's decline from the Golden Age to the terrible time preceding the flood:

> *Then came the Age of Iron*
> *And from it poured the very blood of evil:*
> *Pity, Faith, Love and Truth changed to Deceit,*
> *Violence, the Tricks of Trade, Usury, Profit;*
> *Then land, once like the gift of sunlit air,*
> *Was cut in properties, estates, and holdings;*
> *Not only crops were hoarded; men invaded*
> *Entrails of earth down deeper than the river*
> *Where Death's shades weave in darkness underground;*
> *There in his sacred mines*
> *All that drives men to avarice and murder*
> *Shone in the dark: the loot was dragged to light*
> *And War, inspired by curse of iron and gold,*
> *Lifted blood-clotted hands and marched the earth.*

I paused, shuddering slightly. I wondered if Drusus found the image as disturbing as I did, but he seemed quite unperturbed and urged me to go on.

56

Men fed on loot and lust; the guest feared host;
Neighbour looked warily with smiles at neighbour,
And fathers had good reasons to distrust
Their eager sons-in-law. If brothers loved
Each other, the sight was rare, and watchful
Husbands prayed for death of wives; stepmothers
Made poison a dessert at dinner—sons
Counted the hours that led to fathers' graves. . . .

Again I paused. No wonder Augustus had this
man sent into exile, I thought. The "Iron Age" he was
describing sounded remarkably like the years of Augustus' and Livia's rule. Drusus surprised me by suggesting
the same thing. "He's talking about Livia, isn't he, mother?"
he asked. "She poisoned Claudius' father like that, and
would have killed Claudius too except she misjudged him
as a fool."

"More of Camillus' teachings, Drusus?" I asked, at
which he gave me a forbearing look, as if I were an ignoramus. "It's in Livy, mother," he explained.

We resumed reading. Drusus took the scroll now
and read to me of the sorrow of Jove as he looked down
from the heavens at the impious acts of men. He decides
to pay earth a visit and encounters the tyrant Lycaon,
whom he changes into a wolf. (Drusus took great pleasure
in declaiming this part, reciting the lines with mock ferocity). After surveying the earth he returns to heaven in
disgust, determined to destroy the corrupted men of iron
by lightning and bring forth a new breed, but remembering
that the Fates had already set a still more distant hour
"when earth and the vault of heaven would be consumed
in universal fire," he calls down water from the sky instead
and they drown. None survive the flood but Deucalion
and Pyrrha.

Drusus asked me to join him in reading this part,
suggesting I play Pyrrha and he Deucalion.

57

It is a touching story, particularly the description of the poor creatures' loneliness at finding themselves so suddenly bereft of the human world. They pray to Themis, who tells them to gather their mother's bones and scatter them over their shoulders. Pyrrha protests the sacrilege, but Deucalion perceives that what the goddess means by "mother" is mother earth, whose bones are "earth's guilt-less stones." Duecalion and Pyrrha do as they are bid, and from the stones a new race emerges.

The stones that Deucalion dropped were men,
And those that fell from his wife's hands women
Beyond, behind the years of loss and hardship
We trace a stony heritage of being.

I was strangely moved as I read these lines. Fortunately the scroll ended there and I did not have to read further. Drusus seemed content, and asked shyly if he could kiss me. We embraced, and I was able to leave before my mood was betrayed.

Oh perhaps it is the gods' will after all to let him live and be happy? I would give much to see him so.

July 6

A distressing scene with Lucilla this afternoon, who came over to announce her intention of obtaining a divorce from Flavius. She wants now to marry another man, whose name is Cornelius Sabinus. It is obvious she is his lover, although she insists their relationship has been chaste. How she met him I've no idea. He comes of good family but I gather he has yet to take an interest in anything but high living. Lucilla, of course, claims that all this is now behind him and that he intends to enter politics and run for a seat on the Council.

We argued all afternoon. It has only been a year since she married Flavius, which she agreed to enthusiastically at the time. When I pointed this out to her she retorted that she was too inexperienced then to make a judgement and had merely acquiesced in our choice. Besides, she said insolently, you couldn't judge a man until you had slept with him. I ignored what this obviously implied about her relationship with Cornelius and asked wherein Flavius was at fault. To my shock she started to relate their sexual history in great detail. I was appalled both at what she said and the fact that she was saying it and stopped her in mid-sentence. Suffice it to say she finds his demands on her excessive and his tastes perverse.

Or else Lucilla is lying to strengthen her case, which I wouldn't put past her. I find it incredible that a man so outwardly sober as the Flavius I know could be guilty of the appetites she reported. The coarseness of her language was highly offensive; she sounded like a harlot. Whatever her complaints, and god knows how much she has exaggerated them, I told her I didn't think she should divorce, at least not so soon. I went so far as to remind her that legally her father and I had the right to take her to court and prevent a new marriage.

At this she grew furious. When I remained unmoved by her tantrums, she turned to weeping and wringing her hands, saying it was obvious that I didn't love her and never had, that I wanted to see her degraded and unhappy, that I had chosen a man who was impossible to live with, and so on. Each time I remonstrated with her and tried to make her listen to reason she moved on to a new charge. "It doesn't matter what you say, mother, you or father either, I shall marry whom I please. And I will not live with Flavius any longer, do you hear? If you force me I will take Cornelius as a lover and have a child by him."

"In which case your husband is required to sue you for adultery and you will both be banished," I retorted, which of course brought on more tears.

I suddenly remembered the dream I had a few days ago, of playing backgammon with Drusus. She said then that she "would not live with him." When I remembered this I felt suddenly dizzy. *Can* dreams foretell the future?

She left after agreeing to three things: that she would make no decision until six months from now, that she would discuss the matter first with her father, and that in the meantime she would remain faithful to Flavius. The latter I doubt, as much as I doubt the value of her promises.

I am anxious to discuss all this with Propertius. Frankly I wonder why I am bothering to put up any opposition. Lucilla will get her way, she always does; it is futile to fight her. We could take her to court as the law allows, and prevent her recovering her dowry from Flavius until she is twenty-five, but what would that accomplish? If as she says she despises the man, how would it be to his advantage to be forced to live with her for another five years? Propertius will not be able to dissuade her; she will go her own way. No doubt this new marriage will be even more of a disaster than the present one. On the other hand, perhaps it will be a perfect arrangement: she and this man Cornelius may deserve each other.

What happens, how does it happen? It wrings my heart to remember Lucilla when she was tiny. She was always so merry, chirping about the house like a little bird. When did she become so dishonest and vain? Did we praise her overmuch as a child, did I reprimand her too severely for her sauciness, or too little? Or was it inherent in her nature, the unfolding of which is determined by inner laws that have nothing to do with us?

"We must learn to accept things which are not in our power; and beyond our power are the body, possessions, children, parents . . . ." How vain such sayings seem today, doing nothing to quell my turmoil. How is it possible to accept such things? I love the child, I love the person she was and must be in some part still. How can I sit back and fold my hands and watch her destroy herself through vanity and shallow opportunism?

My head aches, I can scarcely see to write. What is wrong with me that I should be reacting this way? It is quite possible that my anxiety is baseless, that whatever future Lucilla chooses for herself will be for the best. If what she says of Flavius is true, I should not be pressuring her to stay with him. Yet it is exactly the kind of story Lucilla would tell me if she wanted to move my sympathies. I am unwilling to accept it as true.

I must rest, the day has been exhausting.

July 7

Propertius has convinced me that we ought not to interfere with Lucilla's decision and that I was wrong to oppose her so strenuously. He did not directly accuse me of prejudice against her, but that was the effect of his words. He agreed with me that her choice is mistaken and he was equally skeptical of her accusations against Flavius, but still he counselled that we do nothing. "We must be honest with her as to our own judgements on the matter, which are contrary to hers, but we have no right to impose these judgements," he said. "Knowledge comes only through experience, and the nature of Lucilla's destiny is not in our hands."

"I should think knowledge comes from intelligent reflection *on* experience, not merely experience itself," I objected. "A series of negative encounters before a child is old enough to comprehend and reflect on them leads just as well to wickedness and blind suffering as to knowledge."

He considered my words carefully before answering, as he always does, even when he disagrees. "That may be," he said, "but at nineteen Lucilla is capable of considered judgements, or should be. In any case, it is not up to us to determine her actions, for we do not possess knowledge of her situation and are ignorant of the consequences that may attend her choice. True, we could legally bind her for a few more years and have the state treat her as a criminal, but what end would be served by that? We would be interfering in three lives, imposing on them our will and our judgement, without even knowing that the end we seek—our daughter's happiness and that of Flavius—may be well or ill served by such a course." He shook his head. "At some point, Claudia, we must accustom ourselves to letting go. Our children are originally our creations, but in time they grow away from us. Lucilla is no longer a child; she belongs to herself."

I had no answer to this. He is right, or I suppose he is right. But such an attitude is not easy, as he assumes.

He did agree we should try to restrain her for a period of six months. After that, she may do as she pleases.

How little I seem to have learned in thirty-seven years, and what good is this studying doing me? I have yet to see what I read affect a single response to events in my life. I am told I should concern myself only with what lies within my will, and that that does not include Lucilla. But does that mean that if you see someone sleepwalking and about to step over a cliff you should not call out, not put out a restraining hand? It is wrong to deny that we have influence over others, and the refusal to use this influence has as much consequence as exerting it.

If the study of philosophy is doing nothing else for me, it at least enables me to see more clearly how Propertius' mind works. At the same time it increases my awareness of how unbridgeable the gulf between us is. The ease with which he takes the *reasonable* position baffles, and in some unjust way, offends me. My struggles and failures must seem to him equally alien.

Eutarchus apparently believes that male and female minds are not basically different or he would not have recommended to me this course of study. That women can profit from philosophy as well as men has been the belief of many philosophers, beginning with Socrates, but I cannot help wondering now and then if it is not an activity designed by and for the masculine brain. Propertius, and I suspect Epictetus also, seems unable to comprehend how one can be *resistant* to reason or suspect its adequacy. It is as if a force exists inside us which men know nothing of, something that interferes with our ability to ignore our feelings, to "control ourselves in the name of reason," or even wish to. As if we remain unconvinced that this is desirable.

I wish I could discuss these things with someone. There are too few women here who are willing to take on serious subjects. With Aemelia gone there is no one to whom I can address my thoughts, no one to sympathize with me in my troubles with Lucilla. I sometimes think talking with someone who thinks like I do would do more to strengthen me than weeks of studying our thinkers.

July 10

Much has happened in the past few days. I have the sensation that the world is spinning, but it may only be my head.

I decided Saturday that I would engage Camillus in private conversation, telling myself I should test the orthodoxy of his views. Drusus was with Propertius at the theatre; aside from the slaves, we would be alone. I took Camillus aside after our meal and suggested that we walk for a while in the garden. It was a beautiful afternoon, the air heavy with the scent of flowers, a sliver of moon visible above the olive trees.

I began, trying to phrase my words with care, by mentioning that I was intrigued by the history he was teaching Drusus. It seemed in general to be informed by proper ideals, I said, although parts of it I found confusing. Was I right in believing, for example, that he advocated the abolition of our system of slavery?

He considered before answering. "Not entirely," he said. "I advocate, as you put it, an end to further wars of conquest, and I would extend the present practice of allowing slaves to purchase their freedom after a set number of years, but I do not counsel immediate abolition, which would cause immense discord. It is my belief that slavery as an economic system will disappear of its own accord; it is inefficient, and more important, morally and politically wrong, violating the humanity of both owner and slave. When enough people come to see this, it will cease to exist." He coloured slightly, then added scrupulously, "I also told your son that the introduction of slaves from Rome's conquered territories undermined the Republic and served as a bar to its reestablishment. Because of slavery, the rich are able to monopolize the land and drive free men from their holdings, creating conditions of extreme wealth and poverty which breed corruption."

He stopped, abashed. "Forgive me," he continued, "I did not mean to deliver a lecture. I hope you do not consider my views incapable of proof, although admittedly I am biased: after all, but for the accident of my adoption, I would have grown up a slave myself."

It seemed to me a graceful conclusion. I returned his smile and we walked companionably for a time, but after some minutes I sensed that something was bothering him. I was about to ask what it was when he startled me by saying, in his usual formal tone, that there was something he felt he had to tell me. My heart skipped a beat at

64

this, but what he said was quite different from what I had hoped.

"I realize now I should have told you this during our first interview," he said, "but at the time I did not consider that it would have any relevance to my position here. I was confident, you see, that my personal beliefs would not color the content of my teaching; I know now that this was naive and find myself in a false position."

When I looked at him, puzzled, he confessed that he was a member of the Christian faith, a fact he did not reveal to Propertius when he was engaged as Drusus' tutor. He assured me that he did not intend to proselytize or preach the tenets of his religion to my son, but added that he would understand if my objections were such that I chose to find someone to replace him.

He must have perceived how shocked I was, for he winced visibly when I cried out, scandalized, "A Christian, Camillus, a Nazarene?" Such an outburst was very rude, but I couldn't help it. With effort I composed myself, saying that I was sure he would be perfectly scrupulous in Drusus' instruction but that I wished he had told me about this earlier.

When he made no immediate comment, I asked if the practice of his faith was legal, telling him that I had heard that some members of the Christian religion had formed secret, outlawed organizations. He assured me that Christianity was fully legitimate now, that although under Nero they had formed underground cells for self-protection, these had been formally disbanded. For the past nine years Christianity had been accorded full tolerance.

"If so, I am certain my husband's tolerance will be no less than the Emperor's," I replied, although conscious there was a difference between tolerating an eccentric belief and allowing the holder of it to tutor my son. He thanked me, smiling, and looking at him I could not suspect him of guile. It occurred to me that my knowledge of his faith was based on limited evidence and that therefore my negative impression of the Nazarenes could be grounded in misunderstanding. There were many questions I wanted to ask, but I was prevented by sudden cries of alarm from the front of the house and the sight of the slaves carrying Drusus in on a litter.

He was frighteningly pale; after anxious inquiries I learned that he had fainted while at the theatre. "It was only the heat, mother, there is no cause for alarm," he said, but I was instantly gripped by fear. I immediately sent for Eutarchus, and while Drusus slept, Camillus kept watch with me at his bedside. I could do nothing but stare blindly at the motionless body under the linen. After a few minutes Camillus reached over and touched my hand. The sensation shocked me, and I looked up at him in wonder. He began stroking it, consoling me, assuring me like a child that everything would be all right. We sat like that for I don't know how long until Drusus opened his eyes, and seeing us sat up.

His colour had returned and he claimed to be perfectly well. As if to prove it, he began describing with great animation the actors he had seen at the rehearsal. He insisted it was only the sun, and that I should not worry.

Eutarchus finally came and after examining him pronounced him free of fever, prescribing herbs and rest and privately assuring me there was nothing seriously amiss. I have kept close watch over Drusus for the past two days, but as there has been no recurrence of his cough or other symptoms, it seems, thank the gods, my fears were groundless.

Relieved of this anxiety, I find my thoughts turning obsessively to Camillus. Their intensity frightens me. I have told myself that the attraction is only aesthetic and poses no threat, but I am not sure I believe it any longer. He has touched me. The gesture was made in

66

sympathy, not in desire—the desire was all on my part, I am sure—but it has created a hunger in me for further intimacy.

Yet even to write these words makes me tremble. I fear his growing power over me, the growing power of my own desire. When I am near him I feel my will dissolve, as if it longed to surrender itself. Who is this man that I should want to entrust myself to him? And he a Christian!

They are a disreputable people, given to wild superstition and unseemly behavior, although admittedly I have personally known only one of their sect, a man claiming to be a Nazarene who came to the villa one day not long after we moved to this city. I heard Scribonia refuse him entry, and out of curiosity went to see for myself. I assumed at first he was a travelling beggar, for he bowed obsequiously, I remember, and insisted I take from him a clumsily copied scroll entitled "Eyewitness Accounts of the Miracles and Sayings of Our Lord." "I do not ask for alms, lady," he whined, thrusting the roll into my hand, "I only want you to read the words of our Lord. He has performed miracles; he has cast out devils and healed the sick. Take it, read, drink of his spirit," he urged, saying if I did I would be "saved."

He continued with this at some length, but it was only alms he wanted after all: I got rid of him by giving him twenty sesterces. What he said was a welter of nonsense, the words spun out like speech you would expect from someone deranged. His hair was unkempt, his beard ragged, and as he babbled he was scratching himself and searching among his rags for lice. Everything about him was repellent. Afterwards I only glanced at the scroll he had given me before discarding it. It seemed to me no more coherent than its owner, and I resented any sect that could force itself on other people in so shameless a manner and extort alms from them.

How can Camillus be associated with such people? Although perhaps the beggar was an exception: any faith is bound to attract to it certain undesirable persons who set themselves up as representatives without having authority to do so. I know little of what these Nazarenes actually believe. Their faith originated with the Jews, I understand, although converts to their sect from other races are now becoming numerous, particularly among the poor and the slaves. They worship in the synagogue but do not practice circumcision or abide by the Hebrew dietary laws. According to Propertius, who spoke to me of them after my encounter with the beggar, their prophet was a man found guilty of treason in the province of Judaea and executed under Tiberius forty years ago. They believe this man rose from the dead and made himself visible to them before disappearing again. They claim, of course, that he is a god; also that the world will soon be destroyed by fire in a conflagration they alone will escape. Such is the superstition among the lower classes that many believe this prophecy and flock to the Nazarene places of worship, seeking assurance.

Propertius spoke of the sect in tones bordering on contempt. I received the impression that they were weakminded creatures who lacked the courage to face their lot and instead took refuge in emotional abandon and their strange conviction of the imminence of the world's end. According to Propertius they insist on unquestioning submission to their irrational doctrines without being able to produce a single argument that could engage the attention of a person of learning.

It is possible, however, that Propertius himself bases his judgements on hearsay. Camillus is not a fool, and I cannot believe him superstitious: his religion must commend itself to his intellect or he would not embrace it. I must find out more about it.

The chief reason his god has a bad name, I think, is

that his followers apparently do not extend the same tolerance to the beliefs of others as is extended to their own. They claim a monopoly of truth and believe they must convert those around them to their way of thinking; consequently people of good society shun them. In the capital, every discovery of a slave's conversion is met with alarm, or so I gather from Aemilia. It is a religion simultaneously despised and oddly feared, no doubt because of its insistence on proselytizing.

What if Camillus has been sent here by his priests for precisely this reason, to subtly project his views onto my son, or onto me? Is such impertinence conceivable? Surely not: I cannot believe he could be that deceitful.

It is not his sincerity I distrust but my own vulnerability. It is possible that in my present weakened state I should not resist conversion, even to such a despicable faith as this.

The will, the will: is it of any use in the struggle against Eros?

July 11

According to Epictetus, what differentiates us from the animals is that man alone possesses the *logos*, the capacity for inner speech ("reason") and thus the capacity for self-understanding. We have been left free to judge the impressions presented to our minds and to choose our responses, whether of acceptance or denial. The moral man is defined as the man who chooses according to the divine *logos* within.

We would always choose this way, he claims, were we not corrupted by environment and bad upbringing. He admits, however, that most people have been so corrupted, indeed that the corruption of the individual by these things is well nigh universal. In the process of maturing we come

69

to believe (falsely, according to him) that pain and pleasure are absolutes rather than qualities relative to the will, that the one is to be sought, the other shunned; that there is such a thing as "failure" to be avoided and "success" to be striven for. We are filled with false ideas, he says, which give rise to irrational impulses and illusory needs. "The bad man is he who is false to facts."

With this I have a quibble and a serious quarrel. The quibble is resentment that his sentences always refer to men rather than women, who are consistently left out of his writings as if they didn't exist. The serious disagreement is that the argument seems to me circular, or at least to avoid an important question: namely, how does one know, faced with a choice, whether a particular impulse or desire is occasioned by false ideas or is in accord with the *logos*? Epictetus' definition of virtue as correct action seems to me tautology. Right action, he says, is that which is in harmony with the *logos*, virtue what we feel when we know when we are acting rightly. . . .

As a guide to choice in moral decisions I must say this is of little help. My attraction to Camillus, for example: on what grounds must I consider it "unhealthy" or "in error"—because it is a manifestation of desire, and desire itself is illusory? But why is it deemed so? Is the objection that taking Camillus as a lover would cause pain to Propertius and to Drusus if they should learn of it? I presume Epictetus would say that the proof that my desire is contrary to the *logos* is to be found in the pain and confusion it is occasioning me this very moment, the falsehood it is engendering.

But that seems to me unjust. The pain and falsehood come not from desire in itself but from the fact that it is ungratified. I refuse to believe that love is an error. If it does not partake of the *logos*, what, pray, does?

I seem to be either unwilling or unable to reason as they would wish me to. Epictetus would no doubt say

I am unwell, my "internal speech" disordered and self-serving. That may well be, but it is not false. My feelings are the truest thing I know, and cannot be argued away. If goodness lies in being faithful to oneself, the path of virtue lies in acting on them.

And if a sophist is one who juggles words in order to justify preconceived beliefs, I deserve to be included in their company.

I feel for him love, desire. And anger that I should be so restricted.

July 12

Two deeply disturbing dreams last night. In the first I found myself in an old musty wine cellar, in an underground passage beneath the villa. I was puzzled that I had not known of its existence before. It was dark, but I could make out the shapes of old barrells and discarded pieces of lumber on the floor. There was a peculiar odor in the air, which grew heavier as I groped my way across the room. Then suddenly I looked down and understood. "This place is filled with snake excrement," I said, and stared at the ground in wonder, for it occurred to me that I had never known before that snakes excreted just as other animals do.

When I awoke that seemed a trivial thing to be wondering about, a mere detail in a larger incomprehensibility.

The more I thought about it the more fearful I became (the snake is a creature I have always loathed). I was unable to resume sleep for almost an hour, and when I did doze off it was to find myself in another dream.

In this one I was on the outskirts of town looking up at the mountain. I could see Drusus playing on a ledge halfway up the side. I climbed toward him, calling his name. There was a cave behind him, which he entered, apparently not hearing me. I pulled myself over the ledge and followed. It was dark inside, and again I had to grope about. At first I couldn't see Drusus anywhere, but then I discovered him curled up on the floor in a corner of the cave. He was tiny and shrivelled, much smaller even than when he was born. I picked him up to cradle him, but as I did so he fell apart in my hands and I saw that what I was holding was only a bundle of rags.

I started awake, overcome with loss, and wept for a long time. All day I have been inconsolable, filled with thoughts of death and convinced that Drusus will die because of me. I accuse myself of not having fed him properly, of shrinking from him, of longing to cast him off.

These feelings, these dreams, are a consequence of my desire. I must redouble my efforts to control it. My attraction to Camillus is the fever of illness, which I must avoid heightening. Acting on feeling is not the path of virtue but a corridor into madness.

July 13

When I saw him it was to assure him that Propertius had no objections to his being a follower of Christ. We would respect whatever system of belief he professed, I said (although this was not true: in fact I have not yet discussed it with Propertius.) He thanked me, and I asked him to tell me about his faith. How had he come to be a convert?

He told me it had happened in Alexandria, where he had spent two years as a student. He encountered there an old man who introduced him to a Christian community, and eventually he joined their congregation and was baptized. When I asked about this, he described the ceremony in some detail. He spoke simply, with his usual candour, answering every question I put to him without hesitation.

He believes in the prophet and teacher (Rabbi he called him) named Jesus of Nazareth, who although crucified and buried rose, they believe, three days later and appeared in the flesh to a small group of followers. I expressed my doubt of this. Surely he knew that this sort of miracle was claimed by magicians everywhere in the empire; there was no shortage of stories of resurrections from the dead circulated in the marketplace by the credulous. If such an event had actually taken place, I said, it would have long ago appeared in the commentaries and histories. To my knowledge no miraculous ressurection of the sort he described had ever been chronicled.

"You have perhaps suggested the reason without realizing it," he answered. "The Roman government does not concern itself with the religions of its conquered provinces. To them the Jews, the worshippers of Isis or Cybele or Baal or Mithras are all the same: all nonsense, superstition and 'magic.' Disbelieving, or only half-believing their own religion, they assume that all faiths are equally spurious. Let me hasten to add that they are not morally to blame for this; like so many others, they have not yet been given eyes to see."

I found this remark rather arrogant and asked him to explain. Our natural understanding was clouded from birth, he told me. The will was not free to follow the dictates of reason because of our inherently fallen natures; unaided, only a very few were gifted with the ability to see clearly and live in peace with themselves. Most men were weak, he said, as he was before his conversion.

"But how does your religion give you strength?" I asked, thinking that so far what he said did not sound much different from what I'd read in Epictetus.

"Through faith," he answered simply. "My faith has brought an end to the doubts and uncertainties that plagued me before I joined the Nazarenes."

73

"But through what means does one achieve this faith?" I persisted, desiring honestly to know. His answer disappointed me. "That I am afraid I cannot explain," he said. "I cannot tell you how to find faith, Claudia, I can only say that it is something that comes if you have a willing heart." He paused, then added, smiling, "I would suggest your opening yourself to God but I'm sure you would see such advice as evidence of a desire to convert you."

I looked at him in surprise but he raised his hand to forbid me. "I know you have thought such things," he said, "it is only natural. It is true that we Christians are given to proseletyzing. We believe we have received a great gift, and we therefore wish to share it. Some of us feel this desire so strongly we do not make a proper distinction between offering to share our news and importunately thrusting it on others. In addition, we can really offer no evidence that would differentiate our beliefs from the superstitions of the rabble. Indeed, we are ourselves considered the rabble.

"I know that before I went to Alexandria the Nazarenes seemed to me a thoroughly sorry lot. Few among the educated classes know much about us. Most of our members are poor; many are slaves, even former criminals. We are also set apart by such things as our refusal to attend the Games or to participate in state holidays. As a result, there is much rumor and calumny circulating against us."

He reflected for a moment, running his fingers through his curls, a childish, endearing habit of his I have noticed before. "It is odd, but I think it was because the Nazarenes *were* such a despised group that I first became curious about them," he resumed. "It was only through knowing them and seeing for myself their warmth and joy, the way they care for each other despite their poverty, that I came to understand the power of their belief. In a sense the content of our creed is incidental: it is not by words that one is drawn to the worship of Christ but by the light and warmth emanating from those who follow him. How can I express this? Our religion is a religion of example, not ritual or preachment, although," he added ironically, "I am afraid I am doing more preaching at the moment than setting an example. Forgive me, I cannot speak of the faith of the Nazarenes, only of my own. Our congregation is not fully defined as yet; each of us is free to follow as our hearts dictate. Our only commandment is to imitate as far as we can the Rabbi Jesus' example, and to love one another."

"Love one another, Camillus?" I echoed.

He glanced away, colouring. "I know that it is commonly believed in Rome that our 'degenerate' community practices all manner of sexual license," he answered after a time, "it is one of the calumnies I referred to earlier. I have heard the Nazarenes accused of incest, bestiality, of anything the patricians can conceive that matches their own adulterous practice. But please believe me when I say that the Christian communities I have visited—in Alexandria, in Corinth, in Rome—all practice the strictest abstinence. It is one of the vows we take upon ourselves when we are baptized."

Abstinence! The word struck with the force of insult. Did all Christians take such a vow? I had heard that avoiding sexual union was an ideal among the sect, but I had vaguely assumed it was adhered to only by their priests. Obviously not everyone could make such a commitment—the community would die out if none of the members reproduced themselves. Surely, I asked, he was not referring to chastity between Christian married couples?

Again he flushed. "The majority of us vow to remain celibate," he answered, "but those who wish to have children are allowed to marry. Within the married state physical love is allowed, but both men and woman are expected to be faithful and to remain so until death."

75

"You do not believe in divorce, then, not for any cause?"

"No, we do not. Once a man and woman are joined together in the sight of God, their union is not to be breached."

"And this system works, Camillus?" I asked, unable to resist teasing him, "there is absolutely no adultery in the camps of the Nazarenes, nor even a desire for such?"

My behavior was flirtatious, which he must have been aware of. I could almost see him considering whether to respond in kind, but when he spoke it was grave. "We are not perfect, Claudia, only men and women, human clay like the rest. We try as best we can to follow the teachings of our Lord and pray that our faith will sustain us."

Perversely, I would not give it up. "Drusus is anxious that you should marry," I said lightly. "He noticed that you go out at night and assumed there was a woman involved. I gather there is not. You go to your place of worship in the evening, is that it?"

"For some part of the evening, yes. For the rest, I work among the slaves, helping them learn to read."

"And instructing them also in your faith?"

He looked at me, puzzled. "Is that wrong, Claudia?" he asked. "What I bring them gives them joy, it lightens their suffering. They have so very little, and many are badly mistreated. To be able to trace the letters of their name and read the words of our rabbi gives them some measure of dignity, it plants the seeds of self–respect. How can I not offer them that when it lies within my power? Their gratitude is humbling to see."

A different mood came over me when he spoke these words; I grew ashamed and could no longer tease. I was possessed instead with a sudden longing to hold him, followed by intense anxiety. I fell silent, and shortly afterward broke off the interview.

His beauty wrings my heart. Yet as my desire grows, so too does my fear. Obviously my vows to keep our relations formal are of little worth. When I am with him I find myself seized with delight. Care takes wing, and something like joy seems to bubble up in my throat; colours deepen, the feeling of the air on my skin affects me like wine. The desire to tease, to seduce him, overtakes me; I find myself flirting before I am aware.

How strange to be cast in the role of temptress, corrupter of innocence! Always before in my relations with men I have been the object, not the subject, of desire. I admit I find the novelty intriguing.

If Camillus should ever succumb to me he would be violating his vow to his god. Even the threat of such temptation might be sufficient to make him take flight. I must take care . . . .

But what am I thinking? How ironic it would be if these wretched beliefs of his end up our salvation.

July 14

I made a startling and oddly embarrassing discovery this afternoon. When I went in to see Drusus for our Ovid readings, Camillus was just leaving. Watching him cross the courtyard I was struck by the similarity between the way he walks and the way my father did, an easy effortless stroll with a slight swing to the hips. This in turn reminded me that as I was sitting with Camillus the other day I happened to glance down and catch sight of his feet. The sandals he was wearing were not in the style of my father's, but the shape of the foot was the same, and it brought to mind an unexpected memory of how as a child I would sometimes sit beside my father and stroke his feet while his hands caressed my hair. The memory of this was very vivid, provoking a sharp spasm of the heart. Is it conceivable that these physical resemblances lie beneath my attraction to Camillus?

I dreamed of him last night. I was in the public

gardens in Rome where they used to take me to play as a child. I was crouching in a circle of dirt, absorbed in a game of pebbles, but then I felt someone's eyes on me and looked up. My father was crouched at the circle's edge, gazing directly at me. His face was leathery and wrinkled and his hair and beard were streaked with gray, the way they were when he died. I wasn't surprised to see him, only that he was smiling at me with approval, as if he was proud of the way I was manipulating the stones. I smiled at him and went back to the game, thinking I would show him I could do even better, but when I glanced up again he had disappeared.

They did not tell me until the day after it happened that he had died. I was twelve years old. My mother took me aside and explained that for political reasons my father had decided that the only honourable course open to him was to take his life. He had, therefore, with the assistance of his physician, opened his veins the night before, dying a few hours later. She assured me that he was calm and in full possession of his reason until the end. I remember her saying that it was an honourable death, and that when I was older I would understand it. "You must not think your father did this because he didn't love us," she said. "His act was the highest proof of his love. We must revere his memory and hold him always in our hearts."

That was all she said. I do not remember her exhibiting any sign of grief other than those conventional phrases, not then, not afterward. Outwardly my father's death brought little change in her life. She continued to glide about as she had before, self-possessed, unapproachable, managing the affairs of the household with quiet authority.

It is odd that I have so few personal memories of her, as if she were more a presence than something one could touch or be close to. In some curious way she seemed ghostlike long before she died. I was married by that time and saw her only infrequently; once I was no longer beneath her roof she seemed to lose what little interest she had in me when I was small.

I have been told that she wanted to die with my father and that she was restrained from this only by concern for my welfare. When I was fourteen I learned the circumstances of what happened in more detail. Nero had given my father the choice of suicide or execution: he chose the former, thereby preventing the confiscation of our estates. His "treason" consisted in having been courageous enough to speak out against Nero after Nero poisoned his stepbrother Britannicus. This happened at a royal dinner; it is reported that Nero laughed when Britannicus collapsed and shamelessly continued his meal. Several other Senators joined my father in protest, all of them fully conscious it meant their deaths.

However honourable the gesture, can a child ever forgive a parent for abandoning him? I don't think I ever forgave my father. The explanation given me of his place in history did little to fill the void created by his death, which had already glazed over inside me. What the new understanding added was a residue of guilt, for how was one justified in being angry with so noble and courageous a man? Yet angry I was, and am.

In view of this, I am appalled that I could have so recently contemplated abandoning Drusus and Lucilla to similar feelings, without even the pretext of honour. My longing for suicide last month seems in retrospect unconscionable.

July 15

A dream fragment last night where it seemed to me I was the god Apollo, swollen with desire, pursuing Daphne across hills and fields. Her hair streamed behind her in the wind, and even though her form was a woman's I knew she was Camillus in disguise. I knew also that if I caught up with her she would turn into a tree, I would clasp in my arms not flesh but insensate wood. Even that seemed enough, however, and I prayed to overtake her. Alas, I did not: when the dream ended I was still in pursuit.

I had been reading the tale in Ovid earlier in the day. It is a lovely story, among the most charming Ovid tells. As I read it aloud I again wondered why such a superb poet had been exiled for his work. Do our rulers fear those who prompt us to love?

It was strange reading the poem to Drusus. It begins when Phoebus Apollo slays the great python and demands that his brother Eros hand over to him as a prize his sacred quiver and bow. Eros is outraged by such arrogance and puts him in his place. He refuses to give up his bow, shooting instead two arrows, one (Desire) that pierces Apollo's bones, the second (Aversion) striking the nymph Daphne. When Apollo sees her he is hopelessly smitten, but she flees in terror; Ovid makes clear that it is the sight of the wedding torch that fills her with panic. Yet still Apollo pursues her, offering her his love, his protection, his crown, in vain.

Up to this point in the story I was not uncomfortable reading the lines, but then I remembered the eroticism of the passage to come and hesitated. It occurred to me that its seductive imagery could easily inflame a child's imagination; I suddenly understood why Augustus had had Ovid banished, that he was not wholly wrong in believing these poems capable of corrupting his granddaughter. Works of erotically charged beauty that proclaim the attractions of passion *are* a threat to the harmony of the social body, or at least to the family. I kept wondering whether I should be reading this to Drusus, but at length I gave myself over to the lyricism of the language and allowed it to do its work. I read without restraint,

80

wishing only that Camillus were part of my audience:

> *Phoebus had more to say, and she, distracted,*
> *In flight, in fear, wind flowing through her dress*
> *And her wild hair—grew more beautiful*
> *The more he followed her and saw wind tear*
> *Her dress and the brief tunic that she wore,*
> *The girl a naked wraith in wilderness.*
> *And as they ran young Phoebus saved his breath*
> *For greater speed to close the race, to circle*
> *The spent girl in an open field, to harry*
> *The chase as greyhound races hare,*
> *His teeth, his black jaws glancing at her heels.*
> *The god by grace of hope, the girl, despair,*
> *Still kept their increasing pace until his lips*
> *Breathed at her shoulder; and almost spent,*
> *The girl saw waves of a familiar river,*
> *Her father's home, and in a trembling voice*
> *Called, "Father, if your waters still hold charms*
> *To save your daughter, cover with green earth*
> *This body I wear too well," and as she spoke*
> *A soaring drowsiness possessed her; growing*
> *In earth she stood, white thighs embraced by climbing*
> *Bark, her white arms branches, her fair head swaying*
> *In a cloud of leaves; all that was Daphne bowed*
> *In the stirring of the wind, the glittering green*
> *Leaf twined within her hair, and she was laurel.*

It is a bewitching tale. So bemused was I by it that I was at a loss to answer Drusus' question when he asked, "But what does it mean, mother?"

What should I have said, that it tells us that love is dual, that its twin offspring, desire and fear, are forever at odds, that it shows the pain of one who loves and pursues in vain? That is how it was taught to me, but it seemed to me, thinking of it, that the story was more Daphne's than

Apollo's. It is she Ovid identifies with, her body he enters, feeling his own arms branching into leaves. Perhaps, I thought, it was a parable of woman in flight from her nature. Terrified of passion, Daphne prays to her father to release her from her earthly form. Her prayer represents her choice to remain single and intact, her choice not to be "enslaved". To that extent she is a heroine, but she is at the same time a victim: she does not master her fear but lets herself be ruled by it. In fleeing love, she preserves herself, but for what? Her escape is a flight into death, however lovely its form.

"It is about the power of love," I said to Drusus. "It is a lesson to man that even Apollo's power, or the Emperor's for that matter, must not, cannot, ignore love's force. Eros defeats Apollo, thereby showing he is the mightier, that he can bring about the defeat even of the lord of the gods. That is what the laurel is to remind us of. When victors are crowned with laurel at the Games, or generals in triumphs, the laurel crown serves to remind them not to let themselves become too proud, that even a warrior must respect the power of the god of love."

It was a pious conclusion, but the best I could do at the time. Drusus looked at me in some bewilderment but mercifully asked no questions.

* * * * *

Daphne's father is initially reluctant to grant her wish. He wants grandchildren and disapproves of her chastity. He wants her to love, declaring himself an ally of Eros. It is therefore all the more moving when he relents and grants her the form she desires.

Of what was my father smiling approval in my dream—my love for Camillus, or my efforts to muster my will to resist it? I cannot tell: yet his smile was comforting.

July 16

I received today a kind letter from Aemilia. I had written her expressing my concern about Lucilla and asking for information about the Christian community in Rome. Here is her reply:

Dear Claudia,

It was, as always, a pleasure to hear from you: I wish you would write more frequently.

In answer to your question about the Nazarene sect, I confess I know relatively little about them. All I know directly is through my friend, Sabina, who has a slave who converted. Since then her work has apparently improved. Formerly she was sullen and difficult to deal with; now Sabina says she is pleasant to have around, and much more cooperative.

It seems to me a harmless belief, and but for the confusion between this sect and the Jews I doubt if there would be any prejudice against them. The rumors concerning the Nazarenes are almost all groundless; the claim that they are licentious seems especially exaggerated. According to Sabina's Christian, chastity is considered by them the highest of virtues, and even marriage is acquiesced in only with reluctance. The men particularly, I understand, aspire to celibacy if they are capable of it.

Given this attitude it is understandable, I suppose, that we Romans, exhorted as we are to devote ourselves to the family, should view them with suspicion. But this does not explain why stories of illicit sexual acts should be given such credence when they seem the opposite of the truth. I suspect that our real opposition to the Nazarene practice is that they hold themselves superior to our own sexual behavior and presume to judge us. We accuse them of hypocrisy for we do not believe they can possibly live up to their lofty standards. Moreover, perhaps in our hearts we distrust the ideal of chastity itself. For all the lip service that is paid to it (it is still Octavia we are given as a model in school, not Poppaea), it doen't appear to command too many followers among us.

The primary reason why Christians are shunned by good society, however, is I am sure the confusion in the minds of many between this group and the Jews. You must remember that the Jewish rebellion nine years ago, when Titus was forced to level Jerusalem, still arouses great anger among many Romans, an anger bred of fear. The Hebrew Zealots, although a minority, were uncompromisingly fanatical, and the fear of rebellion spreading to other Jews throughout the empire, some of whom were in prominent government positions, was widespread. Many Christians were originally Jews, of course, so they are the heir to these suspicions of treason.

I think this will diminish with time as the two groups become more differentiated in peoples' minds, and calm returns to Palestine.

Sorry I cannot be more helpful; much of what I have said you probably know already. I shall try to find out more.

I don't think you need worry about Drusus: I am sure Camillus must be a man of great personal integrity or Propertius would not have engaged him. As to Lucilla, I think you are wise to follow Propertius' lead. I know it is hard to accept our children's independence, but that is the way it must be. Lucilla is of age to make her own mistakes. When they were children and learning to walk we could reach out our hands and prevent them from falling. The impulse to do this does not wither with time, or not as quickly as it should. But it is a futile gesture, and one that hinders as much as it helps. It is sad that the knowledge of how to live has to be acquired through bruises, but so it seems. Remember also that Lucilla probably has more strength than you give her credit for, and possibly more intelligence. Her choice may turn out to be for the best after all.

Marcus sends his greetings, and we both wish you well. Our invitation to visit us in Rome is always open. Kind regards to Propertius. I hope the theatre is prospering.

Affectionately,
Aemillia

July 18

I have avoided any attempt at seeing Camillus for the past several days, but he joined me this morning in the garden. When I inquired after Drusus I was told that he had a headache; nothing serious, I was assured, but Livy and the Civil Wars could wait for another day. He told me he had set him to modelling in clay, adding that my son had considerable artistic talent. I nodded, although in reality this was a surprise to me. "He can imitate the work of others with considerable skill," he continued. "He has done a copy of the head of Julius Caesar that is remarkably accurate. I have set him to modelling after life now rather than copies: at the moment he is happily doing the cat."

Camillus seemed in excellent spirits. "I am surprised you should offer him Caesar as a model," I said, to which he responded, smiling, that he had not been able to find any busts of Brutus, which were no longer very plentiful in the shops.

He is right, most of our childhood models of Republican virtue are disappearing from view, although until he mentioned it it did not strike me. In the stalls there are busts and figurines of emperors, generals, philosophers, even of favorite charioteers and gladiators, but the faces of those who served the Republic are becoming antique rarities.

I decided to draw him out on his political views. "You are an admirer of the Republic, I know, Camillus," I said, "but do you not think that Rome has been well governed for the past ten years? Under Vespasian the empire is strong and at peace, and there has been considerable prosperity."

"Prosperity for whom?" was the prompt reply. "I wonder if you have you visited the poor quarters of this city lately."

"But there have always been poor, Camillus," I objected. "In point of fact even the poor are better off than they were. Since Vespasian began the practice of subsidizing grain, no one has been allowed to starve. It is certainly better now than during the years of turmoil before he came to power."

"True enough," he said. "But why do you imply that the choice must be between the turmoil of civil war and the tyranny of the imperial system? The fact that on occasion a decent emperor like Vespasian occupies the throne is not a convincing argument. The choice is not between civil war or imperial rule but between imperial rule and a republican system of government. I do not believe it is inherent in the historical process that a republic leads either to chaos or tyranny: our recent Republic existed as a stable entity for over three hundred years."

"With rich and poor, as now," I reminded him. Why I was arguing I do not know; there is no real disagreement between us. Perhaps I felt it was a safe subject on which to play out other feelings, with silence holding dangers of its own.

"Can it not be argued that Rome is still in some sense democratic?" I pursued. "The Senate still possesses its rights, and the people enjoy basic freedoms."

His reply was to grimace ironically, as if I were a child, or deliberately acting like one. "Freedom," he said harshly. "When men speak of freedom now, they mean nothing more than freedom from fear. They mean protection by law from imprisonment and torture, from the arbitrary dealing out of death by those who rule. Yet they are far from attaining even these: they enjoy them at the moment because it suits our present emperor to abide by the decrees of the Senate, most of whose members are safely in his pocket."

I pretended to concentrate on my sewing, but every now and then I stole glances at him. He was pacing slowly up and down in front of me, pausing occasionally to examine a flower or remove a dead leaf from the hedge.

"Surely that's cynical, Camillus," I said. "You must admit that at least Vespasian has governed without violence and that there has been no outward license at the court."

He stopped pacing and faced me. "It is true that no one has been executed, but Tiberius acted within the law for the first part of his reign, and so too did Augustus, for that matter; that did not prevent decades of rule by madmen like Nero and Caligula, or Tiberius in his last years. Who is to guarantee Vespasian's continuing sanity, or that of the man who follows him? From what we know of the temperament of his son and heir, the future does not look auspicious. We could wake up tomorrow with another lunatic on our hands, whose whims determine whether we live or die."

"Security is impossible under any political system," I countered. "No one is safe from change."

"Who is being cynical now?" he teased, but then he grew serious. "The present concept of liberty seems to me a mockery of what it was," he said grimly. "We think of it now solely in individual terms, and we mean by it little more than the protection of our own skins. We content ourselves with a few limited freedoms—the freedom to read or speak what we want, within limits, of course, about those who govern us, the freedom to buy and sell unhindered. How trivialized since the days of the Republic, and how selfish!"

He had resumed his pacing. "The current definition is one which has renounced any hope of reclaiming the right to share in power. It does not represent any longer the ideal of collective self-determination but merely the negative wish to remain personally secure as long as one obeys the imperial decrees. It is an illusory freedom, granted because it does not threaten change.

"Should we call it realism, prudence, or cowardice to settle for this bastardization of our ancestors' ideals? I call it cowardice. Change must come. There will be no diminution of the violence and corruption we see around us until people are made to see it for what it is and stop accepting it as part of the natural order."

"I am not sure I'm following you, Camillus," I returned. "Surely there is more potential for chaos and instability under a Republican form of government than under strict imperial control."

But he disagreed even with this. The central purpose of the Republic our forefathers devised was to obviate civil war, he argued, by preventing the differences between the classes from growing too great. The Republic was destroyed when the Senate began using its power to defend only its own class interests, thus sowing the seeds of civil dissension and paving the way for Caesar. One day this would bear still more bitter fruit, and in the meantime great cruelty would continue to be exercised against the powerless by those for whom power was an end in itself.

He fell silent for a moment; when he resumed his voice was still bitter. "'Government by the consent of the governed': the ancient phrase mocks us, the reality corroded by self-interest and greed. It is an ugly thought, but perhaps we are governed as we deserve. It is we who acquiesce in the corruption we daily walk among. We relegate our power to vain and ruthless men, with our own consent damning ourselves and our future."

The intensity with which he spoke rather alarmed me; I had never seen him before in an impassioned mood. Noticing my reaction, he apologized. "I am afraid I have a long way to go before becoming a true Christian," he confessed. "The unnecessary wretchedness of the lives of the poor angers me, as does the imperial system. We are taught in our religion to hate the sin and love the sinner, but our Rabbi was unfortunately never clear on the point of whether we were to love the institutions that bind us or struggle to free ourselves from them."

"Aha," I teased. "So the Roman government does have cause to be suspicious of you Nazarenes. You do wish harm to the empire: in fact, you wish to see it abolished."

At this he grew concerned lest the beliefs he had expressed should be construed as those of the whole of his church and assured me earnestly that such was not the case, that although neither he nor anyone could speak for the many peoples who believed in Christ, he was certain that the only empire a Christian sought was the one within his own breast. No follower of Christ, he insisted, would ever commit violence against the state. "We consider all human creatures, even the most sadistic centurions, our brothers," he said. "We believe we have a duty to work for change, but we are taught that we must never return evil for evil."

To demonstrate his point he told me a golden tale about his Rabbi's arrest. It seems that the man they call the Christ was holding vigil with his followers in their mountain retreat the night of his arrest. One of the followers, trying to prevent his master's detention, stepped forward and with his sword sliced off the ear of one of the Roman guards. Instantly the Rabbi reproved him, and reaching out his hand, healed the wound. "Put up thy weapon," he said to his disciple, "I come not to offer the sword, but peace."

I was touched by the way Camillus related this tale, confiding it in his gentlest voice, as if what he spoke of was infinitely precious. He confessed that it was primarily hearing it that had originally confirmed his faith.

"It is a beautiful story, Camillus," I replied cautiously. "But surely you do not believe that business of replacing the guard's ear? It seems unlikely, to say the least. What happened to the man who attacked the guard?"

"As far as we know, nothing."

"Well, isn't that rather incredible? Anyone rash enough to wound a Roman guard while in the performance of his duty would have been killed instantly, or at the very least taken into custody."

He looked away and didn't answer for a time. "Perhaps he was moved by the Rabbi's action," he said slowly, "or perhaps the story has become embroidered in the telling. I cannot vouch for the miracles that are reported of our lord, Claudia, and will not attempt to. In any case, their literal truth matters little to me. What does matter is the transformation I have seen in the people who believe in this man and try to follow his path. We have former gladiators among our sect, did you know that? It is remarkable to see men who were professional killers renounce violence and discover for themselves a new kind of manhood."

I don't know why, perhaps because I believe that this "alternate form of manhood" had already been demonstrated, by Socrates, among others, but at that point I asked him if he had read Epictetus. I explained the program of study Eutarchus had put me to (without describing the reasons for it), and said that I was finding Epictetus highly persuasive as a thinker and writer. When he confessed slight familiarity with his work, I asked him to read it. This he promised to do.

"Take care he does not convert you, Camillus," I teased as he took his leave. He responded with the gesture of the gladiators signifying acceptance of a challenge, and we parted.

Leaving me exultant. He is as attracted to me as I am to him, I know it. It is only this faith of his that prevents him from seeing it and acting on it. What is this religion I am pitting myself against, and why does it perversely demand chastity of its followers? Perhaps I do not need to convert him entirely, only persuade him that this one aspect of his creed is mistaken . . . .

Why do I write such things? I am possessed, willfully casting off both reason and morality. I am no better than the compulsive gambler whose mania brings ruin to his family. It is as if some part of me has vowed to seduce this man and I cannot keep myself from the game.

We shall win, my wicked voice crows. You are condeming yourself to pain and folly, the other voice admonishes. But sufficient unto the day is the folly thereof. Right now I care nothing for consequence. Filled with Ovid's "soaring drowsiness," limp with suffused desire, I scheme, I plot, spinning silken webs . . . .

July 19

I detained Camillus last night after dinner. We had been talking during the meal about the latest scandal to reach our ears from Rome. A prominent Senator has been accused of accepting heavy bribes in exchange for granting a monopoloy of the sale of armour to the Praetorian Guard. Corruption of this kind is becoming so commonplace that an honest man is scorned as a fool. Propertius seemed tired and depressed, and although he put forward the view that the system of imperial government must yield at some point to a more representative one, his arguments sounded weak and unconvincing, even to himself, I think. He excused himself early, pleading a slight indisposition, leaving Camillus and me alone.

He fell silent when Propertius was gone. To forestall his leaving too I resumed the conversation, asking if he shared my husband's optimism. The prospect of real change, in our lifetime, at least, I said, seemed a singularly forlorn hope. "The overwhelming majority of the patrician class are quite content with the present arrangements, as you pointed out the other day. Those who are not content, the plebians and slaves, are powerless. How can one plausibly believe then that the imperial system will change?"

He admitted that something which has taken decades to come into being would not vanish overnight, but stated that he was basically in agreement with Propertius. "When injustice and inequity reach intolerable levels—and we are surely approaching such levels now—they must inevitably provoke a reversal. I do not agree with Propertius, however, concerning the means by which this will happen. I do not envision a rebirth of republicanism, nor do I have any faith that change will come from within the Senate. Its members are too wealthy, and the alliance between the military and the emperor too powerful for them to exert themselves against it. No, if change comes, it will come about from something that will take place first in the minds of the masses of the common people and then penetrate the hearts of those who govern us. When that happens, if that happens, the Roman empire will disintegrate." He smiled. "But what form of government would then replace it I do not pretend to know," he said lightly. "In that sense, my conception of the future is a dream, a mere construct of the imagination; you are right to remain skeptical of it."

"You see yourself as an agent of this change though, don't you, Camillus?" I pursued. "When I suggested to you the other day that the Nazarenes constituted a threat to the empire, you denied it; now you seem to be saying the opposite. Why should the emperor trust your sect any more than he trusts the Hebrew Zealots?"

He frowned, considering. "Perhaps from their point of view we are a threat, but not in the common understanding of the term. The Zealots took up arms against Rome and waged a war of violent rebellion; we Nazarenes are forbidden to engage in violence of any kind. Our rabbi counselled us not to resist evil but to respond to evil with good. If a majority of the populace ever comes to believe that, and practices it, the government officials themselves will change. The emperors will seek to obey God's will instead of following their own, and once that happens Rome as we know it will cease to exist."

He smiled wryly. "The truth is that any threat we Christians constitute is immeasurably distant and hypothetical: I see little reason for Vespasian, or any one else for that matter, to take fright."

The "someone else" obviously referred to me. "A nice position you put me in," I replied. "If I do not undergo the change of heart you refer to, by which I assume you mean converting to your faith, I shall be classed as one who supports an unjust tyranny. That seems hardly fair."

He was dismayed at being misunderstood, and once more apologized. He needn't have: it was I who was being unfair; I knew very well he wasn't speaking to convert me. I reassured him and apologized in my turn, and shortly afterward he withdrew to attend to his charges in the city.

After he had gone I sat for a while in the fading light, savouring the interchange. I know we can not—must not—become lovers (my fantasies yesterday seem shameless), but I am warmed by the prospect of his friendship.

I read for a while and tried to sleep, but the bed

seemed hot, the linen irritating every part of my flesh. I tossed fruitlessly for a time, with each turn my mind deepening a shade further into gloom. At length I rose and lit the candle. I tried to write, but I could not find words to express the sense of nothingness that increas-ingly enveloped me. Every attempt was paralyzed, suffocated by contempt. My self-concern, Camillus' religion, anyone's pretentions to virtue (including most particularly my own), seemed worthless excrement. What I wrote I do not know—monotonous variations on the theme of pointlessness, barren descriptions of the landscape of guilt. At dawn, in revulsion, I fed the scroll piecemeal to the flames.

Throughout the day I have wandered in a vacant stupor. There is some horror to come, I feel it, it cannot be escaped. I can almost hear it, like the continuous distant rasp of a cicada; it shimmers in the air before me like the waves of heat hovering above the tiles. It is the path of sanity to deny it, to ascribe these feeling to illness, but something in me resists.

Will: I try to fix the word and hold it, but it dissolves into separate letters, empty sounds. I see it as a straw floating on the crest of a tide, absurd in its pretention that it knows the direction of its travels while in reality wholly at the mercy of the waves.

To clutch at Will is to clutch at a straw: it seems to me more honourable to drown.

July 20

I made the journey to Stabiae yesterday despite my depressed mood. The sky was heavily overcast, but the light was silvered by the clouds. Here and there it shimmered in patches on the water, like pools of dancing fireflies. My depression retreated in the face of such beauty. Grateful for the reprieve, I gave myself without reserve to the rocking sensation of the boat and the delicious smell of the sea. I glanced once at Scamander and saw that he was smiling at me as he rowed, as if the act of giving me pleasure made him happy. I returned his smile, and immediately felt a pang of longing for Camillus.

When I entered the villa I was met by Brytha, who informed me that her mistress was at home and wished me to join her in her bedchamber. Clio was lying on her couch, propped against pillows. She looked wan and ill, her face and arms as white as her gown. Her thick black hair was loose around her shoulders, the single curl at her neck seeming to have more life than she. She managed a weak smile and motioned me to the bed.

"Hush," she said, seeing my alarm. "It is nothing, a silly indisposition." She insisted I sit beside her and keep her company, claiming it was boredom she was dying of, nothing more.

She asked how I was and how I was coming with my study of the Stoics. I replied that I was finding Epictetus' language persuasive but added that the more I studied him the more of a hypocrite I felt. His insistence on the primacy of reason was not in accord with my own experience, I explained. "If he is right that the goal of life is to achieve inner calm through perfecting the will, I'm afraid I am doomed to failure," I said. "I am in the sad position of assenting to the rightness of governing one's life by reason without seeming to be able to practice it."

Clio laughed lightly. "You occasionally take flight, you mean?"

I looked at her, not comprehending.

"Your emotions—they carry you away sometimes up into the sky, like Phaethon in the myth, yes? There you are soaring brilliantly through the heavens, but then you become afraid. It is too unbridled, too dangerous, you think, and you experience a vertigo and check yourself. And then you are back on earth again (or worse, in hell), but in either case vowing that in future you will cling to reason and never take leave of it again. Does that rather describe it?"

I was taken aback by such fanciful language. "Something like that," I conceded.

"I would not have guessed it," she answered. "Outwardly you seem very calm. So the winged horses sometimes get the better of you too: how interesting."

She smiled, offering me some grapes from the bedside table. "You will have to tell me more about this some day, but I'm afraid I cannot ask you to stay too long this afternoon as I tire very easily. It is not really an indisposition I am suffering from," she added after a slight hesitation, "but a rather badly botched abortion. There is no pain, only this wretched tiredness. I am assured I will be all right in a few days, however; the doctors tell me I have no cause to fear."

I was astonished at the openness of the confession and was instantly all concern, offering my deepest sympathy. Having suffered a miscarriage myself, I know the pain of an aborted birth. I started to express this but thought better of it, considering that the pain of loss might be very different from the pain of having deliberately brought such loss about. I had no idea whether what Clio was experiencing was grief, or relief at being rid of a burden. She seemed to sense my uncertainty, and volunteered the outlines of her story.

The father of the child she gave up is not Pomponius but a man named Junius, a freedman attached to the estate who is in charge of the pottery manufacture. He has been her lover for years. Pomponius does not exactly know about it, but he knows and accepts that Clio has lovers. It was a condition of their marriage she insisted on at the outset; otherwise, I gathered, she would not have consented. Pomponius is eighteen years older than she, and she was apparently never physically attracted to him, even when they were first married. They gave up the physical side of their marriage years ago. "I am sure he doesn't particularly mind," she said. "He seems quite content with the present arrangement, which is thoroughly satisfactory, really, except when nature interferes and makes inconveniences like this."

From which I gathered that the loss of the child was not a serious concern, or at least that she did not want it to seem so. Throughout her recital I tried to remain composed, although I was slightly shocked at the casual manner in which she was speaking. I told myself it was silly to react thus, that I should not expect such a beautiful, wealthy woman to behave any differently from others of her class.

"I did have a child by Pomponius," she said after a while, "a lovely little girl, but she died when she was three years old. I have not wanted another child since."

She lay back among her pillows when she said this and closed her eyes. Her pallor seemed more pronounced. I pressed her hand in sympathy, but although she returned the pressure, she did not look up. I quickly took my leave, making her promise to write and let me know her condition.

I trust her doctors are correct and that she is in no danger: I would be profoundly sorry to lose touch with this woman just when she is beginning to let me know her.

Although she vaguely frightens me. Like Camillus, she possesses an odd kind of power, the nature of which I can not judge. I am not sure I approve of her.

Curious: I suspect it is the self that is attracted to Camillus that finds Clio also intriguing. Is that why I fear her, that she strengthens and encourages a part of my personality I distrust?

It struck me as an odd coincidence that she should have used the image of Phaethon while speaking of the emotions this afternoon. As I remember it, the story is rather different.

July 21

An unexpected experience this afternoon, which still puzzles me. Propertius has been entertaining a guest from Sardinia, one Gaius Pentius, by name, who is the brother-in-law of a member of our Municipal Council. Propertius hopes this man will use his influence to persuade the Council to give him greater freedom in his theatrical productions. Fortunately he is a pleasant enough person, but he insisted that while he was here he must visit our Games. He had heard that our charioteers were exceptional for the region, he said (which was pure flattery, as far as I know), and pressed us to accompany him. Propertius, of course, had to accept, but I could see that he was willing to let me beg off if I wished. He was on the verge of pleading my health as an excuse for my staying behind when I surprised us both by consenting to go.

On the way there I wondered what had possessed me. It wasn't "duty," although I could have used such justification if I wished to be evasive; a man in Propertius's position can always use a gracious wife skilled at making her guests feel welcome. But duty was not what prompted me. Curiosity then, the desire to do something different? A desire to test my responses in an unfamiliar role, to take the measure of my state of mind? I'm still not sure.

The ampitheatre was filled to capacity. The chatter of the crowd before the races started was terrible, distracting me in six different directions at once. I grew slightly panicky until I realized the problem was that I was trying to listen to all the conversations around me simultaneously, when in fact none of them was worth hearing. Once I stopped trying to make sense of the babble and let it dissolve into a background hum, I grew easier. Then the chariot races began. The crowd now had something to focus on and became a single body rather than a thousand individuals. They ceased their gossip and breathed in unison, like one great quivering animal rising to their feet on the turns, the excitement of each lending passion to the others. At the finish there was pandemonium, the winners beside themselves with joy, the losers expiring in moans.

I should not write so drily, with such spurious objectivity, as if I were apart from them, for I wasn't. I too was swept up in the excitement of the crowd, a sensation so novel it occasioned a small revelation. I saw that it didn't matter whether the money I had placed was won or lost (actually I lost on the Greens, three times). People didn't attend these events for the reasons we had speculated on at Aemelia's dinner party, but simply to experience the sensation of losing their individuality in a crowd. It is a heady sensation, oddly akin to sexual excitement.

And of course it was that which ultimately made me take fright. As the afternoon wore on the heat grew more intense and the crowd more drunken. Flagons were being hawked up and down the aisles and were plentifully available in the stalls. The unity the crowd had shared during the first races was dissipating; boredom was setting in now, restlessness. The crowd wanted more, more variety, greater intensity. I began to fear that they craved a collision, that what they wanted was to witness blood being spilled. They began jeering at the losing teams, whistling, making coarse gestures. The smell of the greasy food many were eating, some sort of fried cake filled with seafood, mixed with the smell of sweat from so many bodies, made me slightly nauseous. This was bad enough, but in the fifth race, as the crowd stood cheering at the turn, I happened to glance down several rows to my left and saw something which genuinely shocked me. A man about Flavius' age, his hair just beginning to thin, was egging on his favorite charioteer by grasping himself through his robe and pumping vigorously, accompanied by shouts of encouragement. He was doing this openly, unabash-edly. At first I was amazed, but then I felt a flash of something not unlike admiration. Perverse and ugly as the gesture was, I rather admired him for daring to give himself over to his feelings, despite what others might think.

Propertius and our guest were intent on watching the race and did not observe the man, or if they did they gave no sign of it. I doubt if they would in any case; one is supposed to ignore things like this. I understand the tenor of the crowd is even worse in Rome, that there couples have been known to make love openly in the ampitheatre while watching the wild beast contests.

My discomfort intensified and I asked Propertius to notify Scamander that I wished to return to the villa. Back home, I immediately took to my rooms. The nausea has not dissipated, but I am thankful to be alone again, away from the crush of people.

July 22

The shocking dreams I had last night have left me ex-hausted and robbed of appetite. The thought of food is repulsive; I have tried to make myself eat but my stomach revolts. The odors present in the dream have haunted my nostrils all day, making even the quail at dinner, which Sulpicia had taken such pains with, nauseating.

Speech has been equally abhorrent. At table I spoke to no one, as if I were under a commandment to be mute. I could not bear to look either at Drusus or Camil-lus. It is night now. I have drunk a little of the broth Eutarchus prescribed and feel somewhat better.

It was a long dream, or a connected series of them, which seemed to go on all night. I twice struggled into consciousness, but the instant things became clear I sank back again into the dream state.

In the first part I was climbing up a set of circular stairs to the top floor of an old, old building, carrying a heavy jug on my shoulders, as if I were a slave. I paused to rest, and noticed that the walls, which on the lower floors were cracked and peeling, were here covered with murals. I could barely make them out in the dim light, and when I did I was shocked. They were all highly erotic, a dramatically rendered scene of the winged god Mercury violating a nymph, another of a woman offering gifts on the altar of a swollen priapus, still another of the god Pan copulating with a she-goat. I moved past them quickly, trying to avert my eyes.

At last I reached the head of the stairs and found myself before a large bronze door. It was ornately carved with a frieze of voluptuous women abandoning themselves to shame. Oddly, I was not shocked by this; it seemed more curious than anything. At the bottom of the frieze I noticed the artist had engraved the words, *Hic Habitat Felicitas.*

I pushed open the door. The room before me was a vast chamber bare of furniture except for a few couches here and there, interspersed with pieces of sculpture whose forms I could not make out. The floor was tiled in a geometric pattern of black and white. The walls were covered with paintings.

When I started to cross the threshhold I felt something touch my face and jumped back. I had brushed against a windchime that was hanging from the lintel. I touched it and the magical sound of its bells echoed through the chamber. When I moved closer, I saw that the bells dangled from the feet and elbows of a small gold mannequin dressed like a gladiator. Sword in hand, he stood ready to cut off the enormously engorged head of his own phallus, which was almost as large as he was. Most astonishing of all, it was modelled as a dog's head; it faced

101

towards the gladiator, fangs bared, as if the two were locked in combat.

My first impulse was to laugh, but then I grew uneasy. When I examined the pictures on the walls I encountered the same confusion. The paintings were simultaneously comical and embarrassing. One represented the god Pan being tricked by a hermaphrodite, another a phallus with an eye in the center of its prepuce.

On the east wall a single large painting predominated. It too was explicitly erotic, but the delicate tones with which it was rendered created a different effect. It portrayed a sunny field in which hosts of children were copulating, tumbling playfully about among the flowers. It was a composition of delight. Beneath it I again found the words, *Hic Habitat Felicitas.*

I crossed the room. The west wall held nothing but paintings of the male organ, some feathered or with wings like birds, some curved into the necks of swans. On the south wall there was scenes of couples engaged in lovemaking in various postures. Only then did it dawn on me that I was in a brothel, and that the pictures on the walls were advertisements of the wares within; the client had only to point to the woman and the type of experience he desired and his wish would be gratified.

"What a remarkable arrangement," I thought. Then I remembered the jug I was carrying. There was a large silken screen in the far corner of the room, where it seemed to me I was to deliver the water. I crossed the room and set the jug down. As I did so I glanced behind the screen, and to my horror saw Clio lying on a couch within. Her legs were in the air, and between them, thrusting vigorously, was my slave, Scamander.

I turned to run but then realized I was unable to move. I knew I was dreaming, but no matter how fiercely I exerted my will my body refused my commands. I managed to raise myself, but after an instant of groggy consciousness I was borne back into the dream.

Now I was outside the bronze door, seated beside a spinning wheel. After a while the door was pushed open, and to my surprise I saw Flavius come out. He did not see me but stood on the landing wiping his eyes with the hem of his toga. I was shocked to realize that he was crying. I called out to him, but he fled down the stairs without looking in my direction.

I got up to close the door and saw at the end of the room, beneath the painting of the children, my father. He was standing half turned away from me, holding up to his nose what looked like a linen garment. I saw that he was breathing of it deeply; then I was shocked to see that he was also masturbating. I slammed the door shut and once more struggled awake for an instant of consciousness. Then for the last time I sank into the nether world.

I found myself on the ground floor of the building, in the ancient baths, which were tiled in the same geometric pattern as the brothel upstairs. The surface of the floor was watery and glistening, although there was no water flowing from any of the spigots. I tiptoed across the room, becoming more fearful with each step. The dank walls gave off a musty, oppressive smell, as if they were rotting from within. My fear thickened, then congealed into horror as I made out the shape of my father lying in one of the pools.

As soon as I touched him I knew he was dead, even though his body was still warm. I lifted him under his shoulders and pulled him toward me; but as he moved I saw that beneath where he had been lying there was a monstrous nest of snakes, like thick, blood-filled worms. I could see them coiling and slithering over one another in an obscenely throbbing mass. I screamed and began running in terror, fleeing the building. I was running through the streets of the city but the atmosphere was strangely thick with soot and there was a terrrible smell of sulphur in the air, a poisonous acrid stench that I knew would kill me. I ran in panic, awaking with a choking, burning sensation in my throat and my head pounding. For hours I could not rid myself of the terrible odor, although I knew it was only an hallucination of the senses. What prompts such hellish dreams? I see in them my guilt over my longing for Camillus, my revulsion at that incident I witnessed yesterday at the Games, as well as the passage in Ovid I was reading to Drusus where Earth pleads to be set free from Phaethon's fire . . . .

But explanations are no use: the last part of the dream envelops me in certainty. It is the same sense I had a few weeks ago, when I dreamed of being in the market square and suddenly saw a wall of mud coming at me like a wave. Both memories are filled with terror, but even more with an uncanny, transpersonal feeling of doom, as if the destiny I am to suffer is not mine alone but everyone's.

Hic Habitat Felicitas: "Here lives happiness" indeed. What monstrous imagination possesses one in dreams? Am I being warned? Are the dark gods telling me that to pursue my present course means turning my home into a brothel and descending to the underworld of snakes? Is their message that loving Camillus will poison the atmosphere I breathe, slaying my father anew?

I cannot write any longer: I am sickened by shame.

July 23

"Every habit and every faculty is confirmed and strengthened by corresponding acts, the faculty of walking by walking, that of running by running. So if you wish to acquire a habit for anything, do the thing; if you do not wish to acquire the habit, abstain from doing it and acquire the habit of doing something else instead. Thus, when you

104

yield to carnal passion you must take account not only of this particular defeat, but of the fact that you have fed your incontinence and strengthened it. This is exactly how morbid habits spring up in the mind .... If this happens time after time it ends by growing hardened, and the weakness becomes confirmed. For he who has a fever and gets quit of it is not in the same condition as before he had it. If then you wish not to be melancholic, do not feed the melancholy, do not add fuel to the fire ...."

Clearly Epictetus' advice would be that if I wish to be free of my sickness, I should refrain from seeing Camillus. He is my fuel. I should force myself to stop thinking of him, banish his image with maxims and precepts, repeating them over and over, thus:

"Education consists in learning to distinguish between things in our power and things not in our power."

"Education consists in learning to distinguish between things in our power and things not in our power."

"Education consists in learning to distinguish between things in our power and things not in our power."

Epictetus believes that the fear of death is the source of all man's evils. "Against this fear I would have you discipline yourself; to this let all your reasonings and training be directed, and then you will know that only so do men achieve their freedom."

This makes sense. But what is the secret whereby one makes oneself invulnerable, what discipline can be exercised against so implacable an enemy? It is not as if it is a conscious apprehension that occupies one's every waking hour. On the contrary, to the extent that the fear of death determines us it does so in secret, behind our backs, governing our dreams, poisoning our view of the future, filling our nostrils with sulfurous flames ....

The remedy isn't working. I can still see his face.

July 24

I received yesterday a note from Clio asking me to spend the evening with her at the villa. Her oarsmen would bring me back in the morning, she promised. "Come share the lovely tedium of a midsummer's day with me," she wrote. "Friends should not be so apart."

She was in the patio when I arrived, lying on her back on one of the reclining chairs, her left arm shading her eyes from the sun. She rose when she saw me and embraced me warmly. I accepted the seat next to her, and we remained there throughout the afternoon and dinner hours, alone except for the slaves and the musician who played for us as the daylight waned.

Seeing her, I felt my spirits lift: she is an enchanting woman. She has completely recovered her health, I was glad to learn; she apologized for being too tired during our previous visit to pursue our conversation. We chatted for a while, surface talk, and then she asked my permission to speak more boldly, which of course I gave. "I asked you to come here because something told me that I could be of help," she said. "Don't ask me how I knew this; I doubt if I can explain. It was just something I felt, that you were in trouble and that you needed to talk to someone. But not just anyone—me." She smiled and poured some mulled wine from the pitcher Brytha had set beside her.

We tasted and drank. The air was hot and still, the silence augmented by the faint gurgling of the fountain in the courtyard and the buzzing of the insects paying court to the flowers. "I don't know how to begin," I said.

"Has Drusus' illness grown worse?" she asked, "has some difficulty arisen between you and your husband?"

I assured her that Drusus continued to progress but did not pursue her other question, which I wasn't ready to answer. Instead I asked how she knew of Drusus' illness, indeed how much she knew of me.

She relaxed against the cushion and eyed me reflectively. "I know that you are about thirty-six or thirty-seven years old, that you have a married daughter, that you live with a man older than you who is much preoccupied with the theatre, and that you have a son who has recently had a serious illness involving his lungs. I also know that your doctor has recommended for you a course of study in philosophers of the Stoic school. That is all I know directly; the rest is conjecture."

I encouraged her to go on.

"From the reports I had heard of you, and from your appearance and manner of dress, I at first concluded that you were no different from the other worthy matrons residing along this coast. But I began to suspect there was a good deal more. You are very reserved, Claudia, and carefully modest, but you betray your intelligence nonetheless." She smiled, offering me more wine. "May I speak openly? I personally have little use for worthy matron types. When Pomponius first told me of your situation, I was bold enough to hope that perhaps the crisis you were going through, whatever it might be, had disturbed the cocoon of Roman virtue we are so carefully wrapped in. (Forgive me, we all suffer this fate). Perhaps, I thought, her 'problem' is a case of a new self struggling to emerge."

She paused, arching one eyebrow. "May I pursue this?" she asked. I nodded, intrigued. "If I am right, what you are undergoing is a not uncommon experience. Something is pushing you out of your old world, but you are frightened of the new because it is unfamiliar. A part of yourself you have never known before, or not known for a long time at least, is trying to emerge, yet you struggle against it. You are uncertain whether to go forward or backward, and in the process you are exhausting yourself. If I am not mistaken, you sometimes wish to give up the struggle altogether: give up on life, I mean."

It certainly wasn't the way I had analyzed it, but yes, I told her, she was right. Her words surprised me, but they touched the springs of trust and freed my tongue. I began talking then, and talked for a long time, confessing my love for Camillus, describing my dilemma. I spoke of my fear of the Nazarene religion, the collapse of my own faith, my dread of death, my grief over my father; even, at the last, of the brothel dream and the part she had played in it. She listened to it all with a wonderful neutrality, refraining from comment but encouraging me to go on when I hesitated or stopped altogether. Throughout my recital she silently urged me to eat of the delicious dishes we were served and kept my wineglass full. When at last I ceased, she said nothing for a time but studied me thoughtfully. Only after cakes and fruit had been served and the slaves had retired was she forthcoming.

She began with an unexpected question. "I wonder if it is my abortion or my love affair with Junius that you disapprove of?" she asked. I gathered she was referring to my dream, but it seemed an odd detail with which to begin. I was somewhat taken aback by her directness, but the consequence was that I did not bother with pretense (a relief, really). "Both," I answered simply.

"Clearly so. From the dream I gather some part of you thinks of me as a whore. Which is perfectly all right," she added, "the problem is your attitude towards 'whoring' and the fact that you choose to call it that. The dream has obviously frightened you. You also feel guilty, both of which emotions you transfer onto the snakes you find coiling in the pool. The snakes in turn are connected in your mind with your father."

She drank of her wine and looked at me, tilting her head to one side. "May I be so bold as to offer an interpretation of this dream? There are many ways to interpret dreams, you know, many ways to think of them. I do not

108

know whether you are familiar with the religion of Isis, but the serpent is considered by them an emblem sacred to her. It is the emblem both of sexual love and eternal life."

I looked at her curiously. She put down her glass and leaned forward, looking directly into my eyes. I was struck by her beauty but felt faintly frightened, as if she was weaving a net with which to ensnare me.

"What is it that lives and never dies?" she asked softly. "The seed, the grain that is continuously reborn from the earth. The serpent is the emblem of the sacred phallus of Osiris, the bearer of this seed. In the Isaic religion, the act of love is the celebration of immortality. I am suggesting that the shame and fear you feel in the dream represent a denial of love, and specifically a denial of your love for your father."

I stared at her, not at all sure that I understood. "You seem to be equating paternal love and carnal love," I objected. "Surely they are very different."

"Only if you choose to see them so." She frowned, then took a new tack. "Let us leave the dream for a while and come back to your present dilemma. You say you are attracted to Camillus but fear his potential power over you. You feel guilty at the prospect of being unfaithful to your husband, which you perceive as a betrayal, not only of Propertius but of your son and your father as well. This is a very real conflict, and the suffering it is causing is understandable. Nevertheless, it seems to me largely unnecessary. I agree with the philosophers Eutarchus has set you to read that suffering comes from errors of the mind, but I disagree about the nature of that error. It seems to me your confusion is a result of listening to what you have been taught rather than listening to your own heart.

"It is instructive to reflect on what they teach us, Claudia. From our earliest years in school, what are the models we are offered as images of what women should be? First they give us Cornelia, modest and chaste, saying of her sons, 'These are my jewels.' Now what is being stated here? That a woman's only embellishment should be her children, that she should deck herself out in nothing but the matronly role. We are to see ourselves first and foremost as mothers. From every corner we are exhorted to bear children, especially male children—for the emperor's armies, really, although of course they don't put it that way. Instead they wrap it up in a silken package and call it 'fulfillment' or 'acting in accordance with our nature.' Our true happiness, we are told, lies in self-sacrifice. The stability of the state, even the balance of the universe, are said to depend on it."

She laughed. "In addition to matron Cornelia, who else are we given to emulate? Our famous Lucretia, who after being raped kills herself in the presence of her father and brother, thereby setting a pattern for centuries of Roman women to commit suicide with, or before, their husbands. It is as if our chief end on earth is to be dutiful and die. Do you remember the story of Arria and the 'noble' example she set for Caecina Paetus? Plunging the dagger in her breast, saying, 'See, husband, it does not hurt'"?

She mimicked the gesture with a wry grimace. "What do these images tell us, Claudia, how do they shape our conceptions of ourselves? They tell us that we are not independent beings who should seek our own destiny but that we are subject to the destiny of those we marry. They tell us that our happiness lies in submission to their will, their values. Above all they tell us that sensual pleasure is suspect, that our sexuality should be strictly confined to the ends of reproduction and that to behave otherwise is 'selfish.'"

"If you are in search of a faith, Claudia, as you seem to be," she smiled, pouring another glass of wine, "may I offer for your consideration my own, which you

110

must know by now is that of our Egyptian Isis." She waved her glass in the direction of the shrine at the end of the garden.

I felt a tremor of apprehension when she said this but endeavoured to conceal it. I told her that I knew little of her faith and asked if she would explain.

"Let me explain first what I mean by belief," she replied. "I do not believe in Isis in the sense that I believe that there is a female person of that name sitting on a throne in the sky controlling us, nor do I subscribe to the ideology of her priests and their complicated initiation ceremonies—I took part in them once in Rome, but that is another story. I do, however, believe in what Isis stands for, which is the principle of love. Isis is the creator of all things, mother of all things. She cares for her creation, us, her children. It is not our part to question her design, but neither is it hers to punish us for what we are. She represents compassion and forgiveness, but also sensuality and bodily pleasure. Isis invites us to desire, not denial; in contrast to the Nazarenes with their counsels of chastity, she commands us to make ourselves freely available to whoever approaches in genuine need."

She smiled at me mischievously and waved her wineglass. "Isis resurrected Osiris from the dead by making love to him, did you know that? Now there's a rebirth myth one can take to heart."

I smiled uncertainly, wondering if she was drunk. By now we were finishing our meal. I was fascinated by what she was saying, but the wine and the highly spiced food had made me dizzy. I was also bothered by an unpleasant ringing in my ears which made me long for silence. Clio seemed to sense this and stood up, proposing that we take a stroll through the grounds. Darkness was gathering, but there was a clear moon shedding light enough to see by. We walked slowly, listening to the sound of the birds settling in for the night, enjoying the mild soft breezes.

At length we stopped to rest at the edge of a cypress grove. When we had settled, she spoke again of her faith. It is gaining widespread acceptance in Rome, I was told, and not only in Rome but throughout the empire, appealing as much to men as to women. "Men too need a female deity," she said, "a god that combines the principles of sensuality and compassion. It is perhaps hard for some of our male followers to utter our prayer praising Isis 'because she has made the power of women equal to that of men,' but more and more men, consuls, Senators, even Vespasian himself, are paying regular visits to the Iseum and granting Isis homage. Only the Army, with their worship of that bestial Mithras, seems immune to Her charms."

She grimaced. "In this they are the true heirs of Augustus, who forbade Her temples within Rome's gates. Quite natural that he should consider Her an enemy, of course: Cleopatra's ships came close to destroying him at Actium, and in Egypt Cleopatra was worshipped as Isis reborn. But even with all his edicts he only succeeded in banishing the Iseums to the suburbs. Now they are back in the center of the city, only a few streets from the palace itself."

I gathered she thought this a very positive sign. She went on to argue that it was largely the religion of Isis that guaranteed the present freedoms Roman women enjoyed, which we would lose if our rulers embraced exclusively masculine deities. Without the right of divorce and the right to maintain our property, she claimed, our independence would vanish. "A major objection I have to both the Nazarene and Jewish faiths is that they take from women the right of divorce—which is to say, that they take from us our freedom of choice. Isis is the goddess of freedom, and freedom, dear lady, is what I presume it is all about."

112

"What life is all about?" I returned.

"Yes. Freedom to choose, to change, to be what one wants. It seems to me the first prerequisite of happiness." She smiled, plucking a flower from the tangle of grasses we were sitting on and putting it in my hair. "If I were you, I should not hesitate to take this Camillus as a lover," she said. "I should not hesitate to 'corrupt' him. To my thinking, it would not be corruption but liberation. And instead of fearing that you will be converted to his faith in the encounter, perhaps you should try some converting yourself. In my view Christianity is an enemy: it represents a dangerous, regressive trend."

I was startled by this and once more asked her to elaborate.

"I have had some experience with Christians," she said thoughtfully, "and even more with Jews. They each possess attactions, although I personally find the Hebrew world view more appealing than that of the Christian. My objection to both of them lies, as I said, in their attitude toward women. There is a Jewish prayer that some of the men utter in the morning, thanking god in effect for not making them women. That speaks worlds, don't you think? The Hebrew women worship in a separate part of their temples, and it seems questionable whether in the afterlife they are to be accorded anything but Gehenna."

"Gehenna?" I asked, remembering that Camillus had been raised in a Hebrew family and wondering if he too uttered such a prayer.

She shrugged. "I gather it's a nebulous sort of place between paradise and the underworld. How can Hebrew women have any respect for themselves with such beliefs? Only those who are followers of Isis—like Julia Berenice, by the way—truly do. It allows them to maintain a positive view of themselves. It is true that women are much praised in Hebrew poetry—Jewish men are a sensuous lot on the whole, and treat their wives with consideration; but on the other hand, they make them cover their heads and hold their tongues and consider their monthly bleeding taboo.

"Most Christian women, you know, were originally Jewish," she went on. "The fact that so many have converted and accept this new rabbi as their messiah would suggest that the Christian view of women holds out more promise for them. But this may be wishful thinking. You know, I suspect one appeal of this god they call the Christ is that his followers can apprehend him with their senses. He is a deity they can imagine in the flesh. The Hebrew god is officially without atrributes; he is not even given a name. It is forbidden under Jewish law to make any portraiture of him, for in their view his greatness would be diminished by any visual conception. The Christians, who believe that god took flesh in this man they worship, do allow portraits. Whether they are likenesses drawn from memory or created out of the imagination I don't know, but there are pictures of this 'Messiah' in circulation in Rome. I have seen them; they have an odd appeal."

When I asked her to describe them, she sat for a time, pondering. "He is exceedingly attractive," she answered finally in a oddly dreamy voice. "His eyes are powerful, almost hypnotic. He looks as if he is in a trance, although it's not so much that he is blind to the outside world as somehow seeing through it, seeing through *you*. There is compassion as well as knowledge in his eyes. You get the feeling he understands you, that he knows your limitations and weaknesses—knows, but does not judge."

"In this he rather resembles Isis," she said, resuming her more normal, teasing tone. "Really, there is something feminine in the pictures I have seen of him. I suspect this quality is another source of his appeal for Hebrew women, but also for the rest of us, even for those of us who are Greek. No, it is not the Christ they worship that makes

114

me distrust the Nazarenes: it is the preachings of the man Paul, their apostle as they call him."

"Paul?" I asked.

"A wealthy Greek convert to the Christian faith who was tried and acquitted in Rome not too long ago; there was a good deal of gossip about him at the time, which I assumed you had heard. Everyone expected him to be convicted for preaching blasphemy, but in the end he was released. I chanced to catch some of his defense during his trial, which went on for months, and he struck me as a dangerous man. I gather that it is his teachings and system of organization which are increasingly taking over the Nazarene congregations. Originally they were all independent."

When I asked her what she objected to in Paul's teachings she answered promptly. "He despises women," she said. "To him we are the Whores of Babylon sapping the strength of the nation. He seems to me one of those who hate their own sexuality and want to take revenge on it, like that gladiator threatening to cut off his own phallus in your dream. I am sure that the Nazarene doctrine of celibacy comes from him; the tales I have heard of the god-man they worship suggest that he knew and loved one or two women at least, and did not deny his body.

"Which is something you might mention to Camillus in your campaign," she added teasingly. "Also ask him to justify Paul's attitude toward women, and why he has ruled that when a Nazarene woman 'speaks in tongues' it signifies the presence of the devil rather than god, which it does not when the phenomenon occurs with a man."

Again her mood changed; she touched my face gently. "Forgive me for teasing you, but you must not hurt yourself by bearing about these negative attitudes toward your own desires. The hallucinations of hellfire and brimstone you experience in your dream are translations into the senses of your guilt over your love for Camillus.

115

They will not leave you until you see this guilt as illusion. Why not listen to Mother Isis, who tells us that desire is guiltless, that it is a part of life, and therefore holy? Love is not a sin; women are not instruments of sin. We are free creatures, free to follow where our natures dictate. Isis asks only that we remain faithful to ourselves and not deny or devalue what we are. She commands us not to guilt and suffering, but to freedom and play."

She gave a tinkling laugh. "Come," she said, "we must go back, or you will begin to suspect that my designs to convert you are worse than Camillus'. It is late, I'm sure you are tired. But may I make a suggestion? Pay a visit to my Iseum before you retire. Go inside and say hello, kneel down and make a wish. It may be you will find there the answer you have been looking for in the library."

We retraced our steps to the patio, where she took her leave. "Brytha will show you to your room when you are ready to sleep," she said, and with a kiss bade me good night.

The shrine was quite small, illuminated by hanging oil lamps, which were lit. In vaulted niches on either side there were two statues, on the center wall a large painting picturing Her wreathed with lotus. She wore a yellow robe and a blue mantle and held in one hand a cornucopia. The painting was bordered by a freize of shrubs and flowers, through which myriad small animals could be seen.

The first statue, in the niche to my left, portrayed her with the infant Horus sheltered in her arms. On the wall behind were emblems of her divinity: the lotus, the crescent moon, the star. Her expression and the gentle tilt of her head seemed to convey infinite tenderness. In the other niche she was also seated, but here her head was wreathed with a coiled asp and her foot rested on the head of a crocodile. She held in her right hand the ankh, in her left a phallus in the shape of a child.

116

I examined each figure in turn, expecting to be moved, but to my surprise I was not. The images in the shrine were of interest, but they remained objects of an alien world. I confess the second statue made me uncomfortable; I did not know whether I found the conflation of child with phallus humorous or merely baffling. I started to go outside but then remembered Clio's suggestion to "kneel down and make a wish." Accordingly I knelt, facing the painting.

At first I felt only foolishness and falsehood and wondered what witchcraft or superstition I would fall prey to next. The lamps cast flickering shadows on the walls, making the features of the goddess seem to move and subtly change expression. "Make a wish," Clio had said, and words unexpectedly formed in my mind. "Grant me calmness of soul and release from confusion," I prayed, and bowed my head before her.

I waited for a few minutes, during which nothing happened. (Not that I expected it to.) I left soon after, surprised to perceive that despite my disbelief I felt oddly soothed. When I emerged, Brytha escorted me to my chamber, where I spent the night in dreamless sleep.

Early this morning Clio and I breakfasted together. She did not ask me what I had experienced at the shrine, or even if I had gone there, and I did not volunteer it. She is leaving this afternoon for Rome. She misses Pomponius, she said. "We are no longer lovers, but we are still the closest of friends; I do not enjoy being away from him. I will miss you," she added. "I am eager to know the outcome of your struggle. Please write to me when things are resolved. Let me warn you, though, that my bets are on Isis. In the serpent versus dove contest my money is always on the serpent."

"Perhaps neither will win, Clio," I answered. "Perhaps I am destined to live torn between the two."

She shook her head. "It will end one way or the

other. Such contests must, otherwise they would wear us out. Your dilemma, I think, is that you can't decide which is which. Your body tells you one thing, your mind a second, and no doubt your soul a third. How to decide between them will determine who you are, and who you will be for some time to come. I have already offered my advice, Claudia, which is that I think you should express yourself openly to Camillus and let him make his choice. I see utterly no reason not to: you are not helping your husband or your son by taking refuge in illness, or making yourself any happier. As to your 'crisis of faith,' I would listen neither to the Nazarenes nor the Stoics. Your despair will resolve itself if you simply relax and follow your senses. When life seems barren, it seems to me more sensible to examine the state of one's own juices before embarking on the seas of philosophy."

I laughed, seduced as always by the way she expresses herself. Her counsel was very persuasive, and on the way home I reflected on what she said, turning it over, savoring it. But objections arose that did not occur to me when I was in her presence, under her spell. The way she simply brushes aside all question of ethics, for example, as if the moral dimension of experience is foreign to her consciousness. Do we not bear a responsibility to others? Propertius and Drusus may be suffering now because of my inability to resolve my "dilemma," but would not the pain be greater if I shamed them by taking a lover? Equally important is the question of what right I have to disrupt Camillus' life. To love me would mean betraying his faith, whether or not I become a convert to it, which in all conscience I could not.

Clio would no doubt see these considerations as illusory. What daemon grips me then that I am imprisoned in shadow? It is small wonder I prayed to Isis for relief from confusion.

Out of the welter of experience in the past twenty-four hours, I retrieve one odd strand: Clio's saying that Isis is the goddess of play. If I was soothed and sustained by those moments in the shrine, it may be because of the thought that insinuated itself into my mind that none of this makes any difference, that the outcome of my poor struggle matters not a whit. It is all a dance, a game, and we obey the rules even if we don't know them.

The rules in my case seem to be that I will thrash about and bring myself grief. Eventually it will end, although I wonder whether I will know victory from defeat when the time comes. Our lives seem to be lived in ignorance from childhood unto death, this too being part of the game.

July 25

Another disturbing dream last night, this one of the family gathered at dinner. Lucilla was simpering and picking at her food, encouraging her toy lap dog to jump on the table and eat from her plate. Propertius, absorbed in his thoughts, was blandly ignoring this. Meanwhile Drusus was cramming food in his mouth as if he were famished, even concealing things in his robe when he thought no one was looking. As I watched him his face seemed to swell, growing rounder and plumper with every mouthful. I turned anxiously to Propertius, thinking that surely he must have noticed, but he was busily chewing and gazing off in the distance. I started to remonstrate with him but just then one of the slaves announced Clio and Pomponius. Clio entered, and to my surprise lay down between Propertius and myself. She was draped in a gown of a gauzy violet material that clung to her breasts; their shape, and the shape of the nipples, was perfectly evident. I was so arrested by her appearance I couldn't think of anything to say. She took some grapes from the table and

then she and Propertius began taking turns tossing them to
Drusus, who was catching them and adding them to his
plate. I was amazed at such behavior, and even more
amazed that Propertius was engaging in it. I was immediately jealous that Clio should be playing games with both
my son and my husband and indignantly threw down my
napkin. I was still angry when I woke up.

I suspect it is time for my monthly bleeding.

I felt so cheated in the dream, so shut out. It was
horrible to see Drusus gorging himself. I wonder why I
picture him so negatively? In the past few weeks we have
been more relaxed with each other, much more natural in
our interactions.

I have not had occasion to see Camillus alone for
days. Things seem in a state of suspension.

After dinner this evening Propertius and I went for
a walk. I received a message last night from Flavius which
assured me that Lucilla's desire for a divorce was mutual
and that he had given his consent. He wanted my daughter's happiness, he said, and now that love was dead
between them he doubted if life for either of them would be
"felicitous," as he put it, if they stayed together.

He has communicated with Propertius detailing
the terms for the division of the dowry. Propertius consid-
ers the settlement proposal unobjectionable: what Lucilla
brought into the marriage she will take out, her entire
dowry plus the bridal and betrothal gifts, and a reasonable
cash payment where division of the property is undesirable. "Our daughter can have no complaints," he said.
"She is being treated with utmost fairness."

I held my tongue when he said this, for it seemed
to me she was being treated with more than fairness. Such
action speaks well of Flavius, too well if Lucilla's reports of
him are to be believed—unless her accusations are true,
and his fear that she would publicize his sexual peculiari-
ties is what accounts for the handsome settlement.

120

I asked Propertius what his judgement of Flavius was. "I try not to make judgments with insufficient information," was his answer, adding that he preferred to believe that the man to whom we gave our daughter was honourable, even if that meant that Lucilla has been lying.

"Why is it more important to believe a man honourable than a woman deceitful?" I asked.

He patted my hand, saying "I am sorry, my dear, I didn't mean that. Actually I would prefer the whole situation to be over and done with. It is unpleasant and reflects ill of everyone concerned." He sighed heavily, shaking his head. I noticed he was walking more slowly than usual and asked if he was feeling well. He protested that he was, although admitting he was unusually tired. Clearly the new production at the theatre is weighing on him.

They are doing *Octavia*, a tragedy set in Nero's time that has recently played to good houses in Rome. Propertius says it is similar in style to Seneca, but with more dramatic action than one ususally finds in Seneca. I am rather curious to see it; it is unusual for contemporary tragedy to draw a large audience. The production is scheduled to open early next month, but Propertius is having trouble with the actress playing Poppaea. I gather she is exceedingly temperamental: "willful," Propertius called her. She has taken as a lover the chief mime who performs during the interludes.

Curious the way the word "willful" is considered pejorative for a woman, but is used in approbation of a man.

Neither of us wanted to pursue the subject of Lucilla. After a silence he asked after my health and if I had found my trip to Stabiae rewarding. I reassured him on both counts but spoke only vaguely of what had actually taken place. To discuss my converation with Clio threatened to bring up the subject of Camillus, nor did I feel safe in mentioning Isis. I grew sharply aware of how enlarged

121

the area of falsehood between Propertius and myself had become, and felt deeply how hateful it was. I almost gave in to the temptation to cut through the tangle by saying outright, "Propertius my dear, please tell me whether you would mind if I took a lover."

But of course he would, even if he gave permission; he would feel his manhood violated and blame himself. My request for freedom would be granted, I have no doubt, he would not intrude his pain on me or heap me with reproach, but in his heart he would be torn. He assumes I am getting better, whereas I am only improving my skill at dissembling.

There would be no gain if he were to know, only an increase in confusion for all concerned. Or so I rationalized, and let the moment pass.

I have been reading the scroll Clio sent back with me, a long historical essay by Plutarch on the worship of Isis. It is indeed an ancient religion, which has existed for countless centuries. I confess I find its myths extremely evocative, but I feel about them as I do about the stories of Ovid. They have an elusive, musical quality capable of inducing a transported mood, but I am afraid I accord to both the same measure of truth, which is to say, as nine-tenths illusion.

In fact, I can no more conceptualize god as a woman than I can as a man: all gods seem to me inventions. I agree with Epictetus that if the word signifies anything at all it stands for the laws governing the natural universe and for the inexplicable presence of the concept of goodness in the mind of man. God is that part of the soul which knows truth from falsehood; that which makes us admire virtue and feel disappointed with ourselves when we fall short of it. It is our awareness of the ideal.

Much in the philosophy of the Stoics is clear to me until I see Camillus and my senses are stirred by desire. Then clarity vanishes, and into the space governed by language and reason Clio glides, her breasts tantalizingly visible through the violet film of her gown . . . .

A note from her this morning, which she had written before leaving for Rome. In it she included a pamphlet entitled "Sayings of Paul of Tarsus," which someone had thrust into Pomponius' hand outside the Senate one day a few years ago. He saved it because he knew she was fond of such curios, she said. She suggested I might want to confront Camillus with it when next we meet. I have read it with interest.

Much of it is incomprehensible, but perhaps this is because I merely skimmed the doctrinal parts, my eye searching for references to love or the Christian attitude toward women. The references are scant, but their implications unmistakable. "Wives, submit yourselves unto your husbands, as unto the Lord," it says. "For the husband is the head of the wife, even as Christ is the head of the Church. Therefore, as the church is subject unto Christ, so let the wives be to their own husbands in everything." In another passage, referring to the Hebrew tale of the origin of sin, he speaks of woman as having been fashioned by God not to act but to respond. It was the serpent (their emblem of the principle of evil) who "lured her to take independent iniative." Apparently she ate of some forbidden fruit, like Persephone. According to Paul, it was this "independent iniative" that is the source of all the world's suffering ever since.

Outrageous, of course, but really, what can one expect from a Greek? Hebrewed over as it is, it is the same old story of Pandora opening the Box of Mischief out of idle curiosity and thereby flooding the world with troubles. Men seem to feel it necessary to shift the blame on us no

123

matter what their religion, although Clio may be right in thinking things might be different if we worshipped a goddess rather than a god . . . .

I shall take her advice and confront Camillus with my objections to his faith. Propertius is taking Drusus to the theatre tomorrow. I will see Camillus alone.

July 27

We met in the garden, late in the afternoon. When we had exchanged pleasantries, I took out my sewing, and after a few comments on the weather came to the point. "I have been learning more about your religion from a friend of mine," I said. "She sent me a copy of a pamphlet containing the sayings of one of your orators. I am sorry to say I find much of it mystifying and hope it is a misrepresentation."

I handed him the scroll. "Ah," he said after examining it, "I saw a copy of this once, in Alexandria, years ago. But why should you think it a misrepresentation? My recollection is that it's a fairly faithful statement of Christian belief."

"I am sorry to hear it," I returned, "there is much in it I find objectionable. This man Paul strikes me as having an offensively negative view of women."

Camillus looked at me in surprise. I quoted him the passage stating that wives must submit to their husbands in all things. When I finished he smiled, as if relieved.

"You have misunderstood Paul's meaning, I think. The passage has been taken out of context, and I am afraid you oversimplify. As I recall, his exhortation to women is to 'submit to their husbands as unto the Lord.' He then draws a parallel between this and the submission of the church to God. But you seem to have left out the key sentence which follows, which involves an admonition to the husband also to love and cherish his wife 'even as Christ loved the church.' That is the full text, is it not?"

I granted it was.

"Perhaps I should explain his wording. When Paul speaks of the church, he means the congregation of the faithful, those who are bonded together through their love of God. It was partly to demonstrate the principle of brotherhood among men that Christ took on human form and allowed himself to be sacrificed."

He frowned, seeing my expression. "It is a pity we have as yet only the word 'brotherhood' instead of a more general word meaning 'humanhood,' but women are by no means excluded from our congregation, nor are they seen as inferior. As I understand Paul, he is saying that the submission of the wife to the husband in marriage is part of a mutual submission, of both to each other, and to a higher bond. When the woman is asked to submit herself to the man, she is asked to submit to the principle of divinity in him, as he is to her."

"That is all very noble-sounding, Camillus," I said impatiently, "and very appealing as an ideal, but one wonders how it works in actual flesh-and-blood interactions. I did not hear your orator saying that the wife should submit to her husband only when the 'principle of divinity' is operating in him. What if it is not, what if he is treating her harshly, or carelessly, or with cruelty? Does the Christian wife submit to her husband under those circumstances also?"

This seemed to give him pause. "Paul would say yes," he answered as if feeling his way, "but I am not sure I agree with him. To accept his argument entails accepting his belief that the afterlife is more important than this present one, and that I find hard to do. From the accounts of the men who travelled with him, our Lord spoke rarely, if ever, of an afterlife. Indeed, at times he seemed to deny

125

it, saying that the kingdom of heaven was within each man's breast. I do not believe he intended suffering as a way of life for mankind, nor do I think it is good for the soul . . . ."

He grimaced and broke off. "I am digressing," he said ruefully, "to answer your question more directly, no, I do not think a wife should submit to a cruel husband. If he has demonstrated by his behavior that he has departed from the love of God, the woman is right to abandon him."

Does he know how his words make me want to swoon sometimes with desire? I could feel my opposition dissolving as he spoke, together with my heart. Nevertheless I held my ground. "He still seems to me a misogynist," I said, "blaming women for the sins of the world. Surely you see how unfair that is?"

He reflected only an instant before defending himself. "Are you not oversimplifying?" he asked. "Both our first parents were equally disobedient, equally 'at fault.' They turned their hearts from God to listen to the voice of their own vanity, Adam as well as Eve. But it is certainly not something I would wish us to quarrel over, Claudia. Stories of ancient times should not be taken literally. If Paul's interpretations offend you, you are right to reject them."

I questioned whether one was allowed to pick and choose like that in his faith. "This Paul seems to express himself quite categorically," I said. "He implies that all who oppose him are totally in error. According to my friend, he is exercising increasing control over the Nazarene congregations."

"That may be so in Rome, I know not," he answered, "I can only speak for my congregation. Here we take seriously our Lord's injunction that in the house of God there are many mansions. God exists, in our belief, inside each one of us; if this is so, our conceptions of him must necessarily be different. From which it follows, at least to my way of reasoning, that no one has the right to dictate to another what to believe." He suddenly threw me a mischievous look. "Am I getting anywhere in answering your friend's objections?" he asked.

"I wish she were here to argue her case for herself," I replied ruefully, "I feel I have not represented it fairly."

He inquired who this mysterious friend was and I apologized for having withheld Clio's name. "She is the wife of Pomponius," I explained, "it's their library I have been making use of in pursuing the studies Eutarchus set me to. Speaking of which," I said, not wanting to discuss the subject of my illness and Eutarchus' cure, "I assume you have read by now the scrolls I gave you of Epictetus. I take it he has not converted you."

He shook his head. "No he hasn't, at least not immediately, but he has been an excellent stimulus, and I am grateful to you for suggesting him." He then went on to tell me that reading Epictetus had prompted him to compose some religious reflections of his own which he promised to show me. "I have told Drusus that practice in composition is an avenue to truth," he said. "I thought I should follow my own prescriptions."

"I am delighted you have," I returned, excited at the prospect of reading something from his pen. The idea that he had composed the work partly for me made my heart race. I asked when it would be finished and he confessed that actually it was finished now, although in need of polish. Saying this, he drew a scroll from his robe, which I quickly snatched from him before he changed his mind. Once it was in my hands I was torn between the desire to read it and to stay, and said so.

"Stay," he said quietly. "The writing will keep."

Again I felt my blood turn to water. I put the scroll beside me and picked up my needle work, turning my face away so that he would not see me blush. I was trembling, at a loss for something to say. I was afraid he would see I was agitated and withdraw out of politeness, but he surprised me by offering the observation that I seemed much happier now than when he first came and that he was pleased to see it.

Since it was his first venture into the personal I measured my response with care. "Your presence here has been a relief from what was afflicting me," I said, and told him I was grateful for what he had done, both for Drusus and myself. He responded that he had done nothing that he knew of, to which I replied, more boldly, that perhaps it was not anything he had specifically done but that in and of himself he possessed healing properties, like the rabbi he worshipped.

This drew a quick remonstrance. "Forgive me," he said, "but I am afraid that approaches blasphemy. You must not make such comparisons, even in play. Christ's healing powers were a gift from God; they are among the evidences of his divinity."

"But surely there are others who also possess these powers," I pursued.

"In lesser degree, perhaps," he conceded. Then, after a moment, "All right, if you insist: I have natural healing powers which have helped effect your cure, Drusus is blooming because of me, the slaves are dancing in the halls. Seriously, Claudia, you should not flatter me this way. We Nazarenes are counselled to seek humility, a condition I am far from attaining: you should not encourage my faults."

"I do not understand why pride should be considered a fault, Camillus," I replied. "There is such a thing as natural pride, is there not?, which we share with all creatures. When is the stag humble, or the lion? What kind of god would wish us to cringe?"

He frowned at this and shook his head. "Our Christ does not ask his followers to cringe," he said firmly. "Humility, as I understand it, is a quality far removed from cowardice. Moreover, it seems to me that the comparison of the human soul to the animals' is a false one. The animal soul is simple, ours is complex. There is no need for a check on the pride of animals because they are not capable of the same destructiveness as we are; they lack the capacity for committing error on the same grand scale."

"But why, Camillus?" I asked, ceasing for the moment to flirt. "Why is it only human beings who were designed with such a capacity?"

"Because we were granted freedom and they were not," he amswered simply. "Only man possesses language, and therefore self-awareness; the animals possess neither. Humility, courage, power are not applicable to them. They do not live in a divided world: their ignorance is identical to their innocence. We were granted the power of choice and freed from the laws governing their behavior, but our freedom to choose entails also the freedom to choose wrongly. Language enables us to see and comprehend, but at the same time it is the source of all our errors."

I was beginning to feel at sea. "I am afraid I do not follow, Camillus. We are taught in our philosophy that god is the same as the *logos*, the word within. How can our inner speech, which is the voice of reason and conscience, be the source of our error? Does it not come from god?"

He pondered how best to answer, his hands clasped between his knees. "In our belief man was created with the capacity for reason," he said at last, "but he abused it and fell from grace. Our inner speech is corrupted now, no longer consonant with the language of God . . . ."

He rubbed the back of his head with his hand, abashed. "Forgive me," he said, "I am absurd, expounding abstract doctrine like this, arguing with words about words. They only lead us into tangles; it is frustrating that they are all we have."

"But they are not all we have, Camillus," I said, deliberately mistaking his meaning, and reached my hand

129

to his cheek.

He did not resist at first, but when I tried gently to draw his face toward mine he caught my wrist. "Camillus," I broke out passionately, unable to restrain myself, "do you remember a few weeks ago coming to me and saying you had a confession? I beg you to be patient with me then, for I carry the same burden."

He looked at me in surprise, but before he could stay me I told him that against my will I had fallen in love with him and that I did not feel I could continue to see him while remaining in a false position. "I realize my words may have shocked you," I said quickly, "they may even have frightened you, but believe me when I say that I am aware of the tenets of your faith and have no intention of pressing myself on you. It is enough that you know of my feelings, however you choose to respond to them."

As soon as the word 'love' was uttered his eyes widened in wonder. I quailed. God knows how he was seeing me—as a test of his faith, as the personification of temptation? It came to me with horror that he had been totally innocent of my state until my declaration. I shuddered at the mistake I had made and his imagined embarrassment. With shame I saw that I had introduced into his world an ugly ambiguity; it was as if I had defiled his innocence. The longer the silence held the more monstrous I seemed to myself; I was about to beg his pardon and withdraw when he broke it, telling me in a voice husky with feeling that he had no words to express his gratitude, that he was not worthy of my regard. Then he looked at me helplessly. "Forgive me," he said, "you *have* shocked me, and it is impossible to express what I feel. You must give me leave to consider; it may be better if we do not see each other for a time. I do not know."

A part of me wanted to blaze at him and call him a coward when I heard this, but I did not. Instead I assured him that the decision was entirely in his hands (which after all it is) and asked him awkwardly to forgive me for so interfering with his life.

To my joy I saw that I had misunderstood him. Flushing, he rose to his feet. "You must not think of it as interference," he said vehemently, "nor must you think ill of yourself for what you have spoken. You have offered me something rare and precious, which I value more highly than any gift. Surely you must know, Claudia, that the feelings you speak of are not yours alone. . . ."

He winced slightly and stopped. "Enough," he said. "I must not stay longer, it is forbidden. I beg you to forgive me." Bowing, he walked quickly away.

Leaving me in tumult, with surges of triumph (for he *will* come to me, he must, surely love is not something one can forbid) alternating with spasms of dread—the conviction that I have lost him, or that if he comes he will not be the same, that my declaration will have somehow poisoned him. Such thoughts pitch me into despair, but the next instant I am once again exulting, imagining his body next to mine, revelling in the feel of it, longing to cover every measure with kisses. . .

He loves me: whether in the end he gives or withholds himself, there is that, and nothing can take it away.

July 28

He has gone: he has left for Rome. I have read and reread the scroll he gave me. I am even more in love with him now, and even more tormented by what I have done. I shall copy it out as penance, and to console myself for his absence.

His composition is in fact a letter to me:

My dear Claudia,

I am deeply grateful to you for lending me the work of this highly praiseworthy philosopher. Epictetus is a man of genuine virtue, and in many respects there is no conflict between his beliefs and mine, as, for example, when he writes,

> Man, be bold even to despair, that you may have peace and freedom and a lofty mind. Lift up your neck at last, as one released from slavery. Have courage to look to God and say, "Deal with me hereafter as Thou wilt, I am as one with Thee, I am Thine. I flinch from nothing so long as Thou thinkest it good. Lead me where Thou wilt ....

Statements like this make me wonder at times if the man is not a secret Christian. Little seems to be known of him except that he was once a slave in Nero's court; I understand he now lives modestly just outside Rome, where he operates a school like his mentor, Socrates.

I am deeply impressed by the role Socrates plays in Epictetus' work. I wonder if one should call the system he expounds a religion or a philosophy, by the way? At times he seems to mean by the word 'god' merely the forces of nature, at others an intelligence separate from but operative within it. I find it difficult to conceptualize either.

I can, however, conceptualize Socrates, as easily as I can the Rabbi Jesus. One difference between Epictetus and myself is that I am willing to say of both teachers that they are as much divine as human, whereas Epictetus, I assume, would insist purely on their humanity.

I picture you asking why, given these two models of virtue, I should prefer Christ to Socrates. I have tried to examine my beliefs as impartially as I can, and I conclude that in the end it may be simply a matter of temperament. Socrates, as Epictetus presents him, is a heroic model of a man who devoted his life to an ideal. One is automatically drawn to him because of this; but however vividly he portrays his teacher and however eloquent his defense of his beliefs, there is an abstractness, an austerity at the center of his thought that I cannot be comfortable with. The Stoic ethic is unquestionably noble, but I can't help feeling it is an ethic for a select few only. Epictetus' references to 'the gods' remain more a part of a formal syllogism than something one can turn to in one's heart. Because of this his ideals seem to me impossibly high for the average man to grasp, unaided by a belief in a personal deity.

In fairness I should say this is not always true. There are passages in the discourses that are deeply moving. I was touched, for example, by the following:

> Cleanse your own heart, cast out from your mind pain, fear, desire, envy, ill will, avarice, cowardice, passion uncontrolled. These things you cannot cast out, unless you look to God alone, on Him alone set your thoughts, and consecrate yourself to His commands. If you wish for anything else, with groaning and sorrow you will follow what is stronger than you, ever seeking peace outside you, and never able to be at peace: for you seek it where it is not, and refuse to seek it where it is.

There are several passages like this which stir the spirit, but on the whole Epictetus appeals largely to the reason.

I see that my objections to his beliefs are twofold: first that the ethic he holds up for us is too lofty for the average man in his weakness to attain, and second that he reduces the complexity of human experience to a false simplicity. He assumes too easily that we are creatures governed by reason. I am particularly bothered by the way he speaks of death. "It is not death or pain which is fearful," he says, "but the fear of death or pain." Death itself is a nothingness, an unknowing. Therefore we ought to confront it with confidence and concentrate on removing our unrealistic fear of it. In reality, of course, we do the contrary. We attempt, foolishly, to fly from death, when it is really our fear of it we should banish. "Socrates called such fears bogies, and rightly too," Epictetus writes. "Just as masks seem fearful and terrible to children from want of experience, so we are affected by events for much the same reason. What makes a child? Want of knowledge, want of instruction. What is death? A bogey. Turn it round and see what it is: you see it does not bite. The stuff of the body was bound to be parted from the airy element, either now or hereafter, as it existed apart from it before. Why then are you vexed if they are parted now? If not parted now, they will be hereafter. What is pain? A bogey. Turn it round and see what it is. The poor flesh is subject to rough movement, then again to smooth. If it is not to your profit, the door stands open: if it is to your profit, bear it. . . ."

How easily these lofty words brush aside man's wretchedness and suffering! Death, pain, confusion—all are classed as childishness, an ignorance of the proper use of the will. It may be so. But of what use is such knowledge to those who suffer?

He gives himself away, I think, by saying a little further on that only the educated are free. By "educated" he ostensibly means those who have been trained to concern themselves with that which lies within the purview of the will, but unwittingly, it seems to me, he lays bare the prejudice of his class. His philosophy is designed by and suited to the patricians, those who have sufficient leisure and means to devote their time to perfecting their wills; or even more narrowly, to the small class of wealthy men born with a gift for abstract thought and a weakness of the passions that makes them relatively immune to their call.

It strikes me thus as a philosophy of and for the

elite, although perhaps my charge is unjust: both Socrates and Epictetus knew what it was to work with their hands. One cannot help admiring Epictetus, indeed, there are times when admiration swells to affection, but in the end I find myself resisting him. Is there not a selfishness at the core of this thought that we should struggle against? Man's sole purpose is described as the achievement of inner peace through making his will consonant with the world of nature. Praiseworthy as this might be, it seems to me insufficient, even if it were attainable by more than a chosen few. What attracts me to the Christian faith is the belief that it is not our own souls merely that should be our concern but that of our brothers also. It is not enough to live 'in calm content and singular purity of mind.' We exist as part of one another, as part of a larger community.

Epictetus' solitary ethic ultimately leaves the heart unsatisfied. I know this is true for me, and believe that it must be true in some part for others also. I do not believe that I alone hunger for something more transcendent than is offered in our schools. It seems to me there is a longing in every man's heart for the rapture of union with something greater than himself.

'There is only one commandment I give to you, and that is that you love one another.' This to me is the essence of the message of our Lord. It is a commandment that stirs me to follow, a goal I find of greater worth than the achievement of inner peace, which is in the end only the pursuit of selfish happiness, however nobly defined.

I have one further quarrel with Epictetus, who at one point says of Socrates:

He was like one playing at ball. What then was the ball that he played with? Life, imprisonment, exile, taking poison. . . . These were the things he played with, but none the less he played and tossed the ball with balance. So ought we to play the game, so to speak, with all possible care and skill, but treat the

135

ball itself as indifferent.

That is something I am reluctant to do, "treat the ball itself as indifferent." It seems to me an empty goal, one that ignores the craving of man's heart for justice. My desire is to live life with passion and humility, doing what I can to mitigate the suffering and ignorance I encounter along the way.

Epictetus claims that freedom is secured not by the fulfilling of men's desires, but by the removal of desire. If that is so, few men are free, or can ever aspire to be. How can a hungry man control his craving for food? Epictetus has a more exalted image of man than I. Where he sees strength, I see, in myself and in others, only weakness. His philosophy may hold for those upright souls who need no other guide than reason to sustain them, but the majority of us, even those with sufficient bread, walk crookedly, in darkness, and need God's light to help us on our way.

I do not mean to end in condemnation, however. There is much in this man to take to heart, and I thank you again for giving me an opportunity to read him. Epictetus claims that the first thing one must learn in philosophy is that the gods exist and provide for the universe, and that the second is to learn their true nature. "For whatever their nature is discovered to be, he that is to please and obey them must needs try, so far as he can, to make himself like them. If God is faithful, he must be faithful too; if free, he must be free; if beneficent, he too must be beneficent. He must, in fact, as one who makes God his ideal, follow this out in every act and word."

There would be no conflict between us if only Epictetus had added that the essence of God is love. Lacking this attribute, which he neglects to mention, God remains a noble but lifeless aspiration, a disembodied word lacking flesh.

Yours faithfully,
Camillus

* * * * *

I was up most of the night copying this, and afterwards slept little. When I awoke this morning I was filled with anxiety. I couldn't eat, and was barely able to compose myself sufficiently to dress. After my duties were completed I started toward the garden, hoping to see Camillus, but I was given a message informing me that Lepida, one of our slave women, was in the throes of labor. I felt obliged to go to her and offer what comfort I could; it was her firstborn, and I knew she was fearful of dying. Fortunately my authority added value to my assurances and I was able to sustain her through the delivery, which took place shortly after noon. I left the chamber in search of Camillus but was told that he had already departed for Rome, leaving the following note:

My dearest,

Your declaration yesterday, which was completely unexpected, threw me into a state of turmoil. Until you spoke I did not realize the nature of my own feelings; I did not see how steeped I was in self-deception. The discovery has shocked me. That I could have so misunderstood my love for you has made me call into question everything I know about myself, and has forced me to reexamine my deepest convictions.

Perhaps I should simply detail as best I can what has happened to me since parting from you. I went back to my room and tried to pray, but Christ seemed far away and it was your face I kept seeing. I longed passionately to hold it between my hands and cherish it. Such sweetness there was, Claudia, in such a fantasy; I would never have believed that temptation could take such sweet forms! But then the very fact that I should see you as "temptation," as an agent possibly sent by the powers of darkness to test my

137

faith, seemed monstrous, something twisted and perverse. For the first time it occurred to me that what I had been taught might be in opposition to truth rather than one with it.

I paced the room in great agitation, at length leaving the villa and walking down to the bay. The night was still, the waters murmuring and lapping against the dock. Gradually their rhythm calmed my mood. I looked out across the sea and I saw your face, and I saw His, and the two blended together, fusing into a single longing. He commanded us to love one another, but we are told at the same time to resist the desires of the flesh. How could he not have known that the two were inseparable, how could he have given such contradictory commands?

The more I wrestled with this the more entangled I became. Plato claims that sexual love is one path leading to the love of God. At one moment I was ready to believe this, but the next I imagined I heard the voice of my Rabbi saying that we must not covet that which belongs to another, that we should love all human beings equally, as part of Him, that to love selfishly is an evil to be shunned. The desire to hold you in my arms kept turning into anguish and I would revert to my earlier sin of seeing you not as you are in yourself but as something offered to me as a test or a challenge. It kept recurring to me that it would be precisely through loving you purely and struggling to transcend physical desire that I would genuinely deserve to be called Christ's follower. Surely this was the counsel of God, I would think, but within minutes it would seem the counsel of the devil. I felt guilty of sacrilege for treating you as a test of my miserable faith, and longed to go to you and ask for forgiveness as a child would of its mother after committing an act of shame.

Such feelings led me, finally, to the thought of Propertius, and I knew then that for this reason if for no other, you and I must renounce any hope of loving each other in the flesh. I cannot be an agent of shame to a virtuous man; it is not right, in anyone's philosophy.

I returned to the villa, determined to tell you that under the circumstances it would be unwise for us to stay in physical proximity to each other, at least for the present. I desire above all for our friendship to continue, and to continue in honesty, but right now it is hard to see how this is possible.

When I awoke this morning this earlier resolution was swallowed up in the desire to see and embrace you. I have therefore decided to pay a short visit to Rome, which I have been intending to do in any case. I recently received a letter from my mother that led me to believe that her health is declining.

I will communicate with you further when I reach the capital. Forgive me if what I am exhibiting is cowardice. As I said in my comments on Epictetus, there are those of us who are weak.

Camillus

* * * * *

I have gone over this letter again and again. But the more I study it the more I am thrown into the same confusion Camillus describes. My feelings swing from pole to pole, desire buoying me up into the heavens, terror that he will not come back, or that his god is right and that our love for each other is a sin, plunging me back into darkness.

When he classes himself among the weak, does he mean the class of men who need Christ because they know their will is not strong enough to resist desire? Has he fled because he knows he cannot stand against me? He will be among fellow Christians in Rome; they will no doubt "strengthen" him, confirm him in his damnable faith. . . .

I must not think this way. Whatever he decides, I

139

must accept it. If we are not to touch, so be it; I will content myself with whatever he offers. I want only to see him, to be near him, to hear his voice again: please god let him come back to me.

August 1

A confused medly of dreams last night, of Drusus dying, of Lucilla turning into a whore, of my mother in tears. Most vivid of all was a dream of seeing flames shooting from between the pillars of the Iseum, a dream which has left me shaken.

The previous evening I attended the dedication ceremonies of the new temple of Isis. After the high priest sacrificed a calf and blessed the crowd, there was a torch-light procession to the docks, where a ship was consecrated. The entire ceremony was unexpectedly moving, stirring in me a tangle of emotion. I longed passionately for Camillus, in imagination clothing him in the vestments of the priesthood of Isis and leading him by the hand into the sanctuary. Clio's spirit took possession of mine and I willed him, fiercely, so many miles away, to come back to me. I prayed to Isis to visit him, to stay with him, I commanded him in Her name to love me and put aside this god of his that makes him fear and spurn the needs of the body. The night, the air, bewitched me. I was seized by giddiness and longed to dance, to tear off my clothes, give myself freely to madness . . . .

In the dream I am punished for my inflamed desires: the Iseum is burned to the ground. The flames devoured the temple, giving off the same acrid stench that tormented me a week ago, only now there was added to it the suffocating sweetness of the odor of bodies in decay. All around me I saw people dying, sinking wordlessly into the streets, their eyes bulging from their heads in terror. I awoke with my heart pounding and the same choking, strangling sensation that accompanied the dream of the brothel. It took hours of forced study finally to rid my senses of the illusion, which is not entirely gone even now.

I must be deranged; if by nothing else I can tell from Propertius' manifestations of concern. At his insistence, I have agreed to see Eutarchus the day after tomorrow. Shall I confess to him the outcome of his therapy, or dissemble my feelings?

I have no intention of following his advice if it differs from my desire, so why should I solicit it? If I am ill, it is willfully so. I love, I am possesssed by love, I will to love.

It is none of his affair.

I shall not feel real to myself until I hear from Camillus.

August 2

Still no word.

I was supposed to read Ovid with Drusus today, but in my agitated state (outwardly frozen, seething beneath the surface) I dreaded speaking the verses aloud, not knowing what emotions they might evoke. I suggested instead, as a treat, that we read together the newly copied scrolls of Tacitus, which Felix has at last completed. I persuaded Drusus by pointing out that they involved accounts of Nero's reign, so that when he saw his father's production of *Octavia* a few weeks hence he would have a first-hand historical narrative to compare it with. He consented, and we spent the hour reading paragraphs in turn.

The smooth clarity of the prose exceeded my expectations, even though I was prepared to respond positively. I doubt if any dramatist can surpass this new historian in his ability to bring character to life. But the story he tells is appalling, leaving one to marvell at what manner of creatures we are that we can produce and countenance such viciousness among our kind. Although it is true that there were also men of that decade, like my father, who gave their lives in protest against it . . .

My father has dominated my thoughts ever since the reading, for it unlocked a memory that has lain buried in my heart for years. The memory has, in turn, provoked healing dreams. I am calmer now, the sense of dread, which never entirely leaves me, moved somewhat at a distance.

The memory recurred as Drusus was reading the terrible account of Nero's murder of Britannicus, his step-brother, a man, Tacitus points out, who had a better claim to the throne than Nero. Drusus read eagerly, in a charming boyish voice earnestly imitating a man's:

It was the custom for young imperial princes to eat at a special, less luxurious table, before the eyes of their relations: that is where Britannicus dined. A selected servant habitually tasted his food and drink. But Nero had thought of a way of leaving this custom intact without giving himself away by a double death. Britannicus was handed a harmless drink. The taster had tasted it; but Britannicus found it too hot, and refused it. Then cold water containing the poison was added. Speechless, his whole body convulsed, Britannicus instantly ceased to breathe.

His companions were horrified. Some, uncomprehending, fled. Others, understanding better, remained rooted in their places, staring at Nero. He lay back unconcernedly, and remarked that this often happened to epileptics, that Britannicus had been one since infancy, and that soon his sight and consciousness would return. His mother tried to control her features, but their evident consternation and terror showed that, like Octavia, Nero's wife, she knew nothing. She realized now that her last support was gone; here was Nero murdering a relation. But Octavia, young though she was, had learned to hide sorrow, affection, every feeling. After a short silence the banquet continued.

Britannicus was cremated the night he died. Indeed, preparations for his inexpensive funeral had already been made. As his remains were placed in the Field of Mars, there erupted a violent storm. It was widely believed that the gods were showing their fury at the boy's murder. . . .

I could not concentrate on the rest, for in that instant there flashed on me the memory of that very storm. I was only a child at the time, no more than twelve. I had been awakened in the dead of night by fierce claps of thunder and howling winds. The slaves, responding to my cries, hastened to my bedside but were unable to comfort me; I screamed repeatedly for my father and would not be consoled until he came. At last he did. He sat beside me and cradled me in his arms, soothing my fears by telling me that the gods were only showing off their might in order that man might learn humility. The winds would pass, he said, I should never be afraid; he would always protect me, and even if he should be some day absent from me his spirit would still be with me. I must be brave and accept whatever fortune ordained, for one day, he promised, I would understand the gods' design and see that all things were for the best.

That day has not come, my father, but I thank you for the gift you gave me that at the time I did not comprehend.

I see now that he knew as he spoke that the

moment was fast approaching when he would have to make his choice between dishonour and death. I find it strange that I should have forgotten this encounter, blocked it from memory until now.

Last night, in my dream, I saw him, at first only from a great distance. He was standing on a hill looking out to sea. When I neared he turned and smiled and stretched out his arms, his eyes shining with welcome. The vision has given me hope, irrationally encouraging me to believe that whatever my sense of dread may portend, I will somehow win through.

August 3

Again no word.

An interview with Eutarchus, to whom I revealed nothing. He clearly knew I was dissembling when in answer to his queries I said there was nothing wrong (I have lost weight, I am haggard from little sleep). "It is obvious you are suffering," he said stiffly, "although the nature of the stress you are under I do not understand. I am afraid I can be of little help if you will not be forthcoming."

To pacify him I told him one of my recent nightmares. Concluding that I was still suffering from fears of Drusus' ill health, he assured me that dreams were not faithful predictions of the future and suggested it would be good for me to take a trip, to Rome, he suggested, to visit Aemelia, but noting my consternation at this idea did not press it. Instead he recommended a new herbal prescription and suggested I add eels cooked in olive oil to my diet.

He also asked about my writing and if I would be willing to show him any of my scrolls. I told him that that was impossible inasmuch as I destroyed each one when it

144

was completed. Once again I am sure he knew I was lying but he did not pursue it. Instead he asked abruptly about the frequency of my lovemaking with Propertius. When I coloured and informed him that I did not think the question a proper one, he answered testily that he was concerned with my health. "You know from your readings of Lucretius, dear lady, that mind and body cannot be considered apart. Excessive heat in the one can lead to psychic disorders, manifesting themselves in irrational fears and phobias such as those you are experiencing. If it is not too painful, I must ask you to decribe for me your relations with your husband."

"Surely you could obtain this information from him?" I asked.

"Yes indeed, but it would be his information, not yours. It is how you see your relations that concerns me, and this he is in no position to tell me."

"Our 'relations,' as you call them, are non-existent," I replied. "We live as brother and sister, in affection and esteem, but our sleeping arrangements are solitary."

"Does this state of affairs exist by mutual, stated agreement?"

"Mutual, but not stated."

"Ah."

He sighed again, placing his hands on his knees. "I would wish it otherwise," he said, wagging his finger at me. "I suggest you reconsider the policy of separate sleeping quarters. It is not good for human beings to go without touch for long periods of time. Even if you do not resume intercourse, I would advise you to resume physical contact with him."

To this I retorted that my flesh crawled at the thought, surprising myself almost as much as he by the remark.

"I am sure you cannot mean that, dear lady," he said when he recovered. "If true, I am grieved to hear it.

But why should you feel so? Your husband is in good health and is perfectly sound of limb."

I resisted the temptation to reply that one of his limbs at least was signally lacking in vigor and said instead that it was not Propertius but the idea of physical contact itself that made me shrink (another lie). At this he gave me a searching look and reminded me that a physician could do nothing if the patient was unwilling to cooperate. "I do not wish to judge you, madame," he reproved, "it isn't my place to do so, but I advise you to take heed. Overcome these imaginary scruples of yours and resume your physical relations with your husband. If you do not, I must warn you that there is danger of folly ahead, if indeed it is not under way already."

I started to object to this but he raised his hand for silence. "I have no wish to quarrel," he said wearily. "You are free to reject what I suggest; I do not make any claim to omniscience. Because I wish your family well I offer such counsel as seems to me correct, but no man can deflect the course of another's life if his will is set against it. The ultimate resolution of your distress is between yourself and the gods. I have done what I can."

There was a pitying note in his voice that I found oddly moving. I did not like to hear him confess to failure, and hastened to reassure him. His counsels had done me good in the past, I said with some sincerity, I would consider what he advised. At length he was mollified and took his leave, although still with a grieved countenance.

I know he is right, but my reaction, childishly, is to despise him. However correct his advice, he speaks in ignorance. I cannot imagine resuming relations with Propertius: the thought of him turns my heart to stone. He represents death to me now, the prospect of an existence lived out in perpetual darkness. Only shutting him from consciousness and turning to fantasies of Camillus lifts the oppressive sense of suffocation I associate with my marriage. Only when I see his face am I restored to light, to freedom. Then I soar for a space, unfettered, but always I am pulled back once again into heaviness, as if I am Andromache in the painting in Clio's reception room, chained to a rock, awaiting my rescuer's sword. Whether he will fly to release me or cut off my head, however, is beyond my sight.

August 4

The courier came today from Rome, but there was nothing from Camillus. Instead there was a letter from Aemelia, who said that she had seen him. It also brought news of Vespasian's death.

Dear Claudia,

As I suppose you have heard, Vespasian passed away a few days ago and has been succeeded by his son. Since this has been expected for weeks and thoroughly prepared for, the succession proceeded quite smoothly. Titus has been unanimously acclaimed by the Senate (his acclamation by the Army was always assured). His father's reign being assessed as on the whole moderate and wise, people have little desire for change, although they hope, naturally, that Titus will discontinue Vespasian's parsimonious policies and be a little freer with the state's largesse.

Speaking of parsimony, I must tell you of the skit at the theatre last night in which the actors mimicked the obsequies at the emperor's funeral. (This, by the way, as such things go, was notable for its comparative simplicity, even though Vespasian was, as usual, proclaimed a god). During the mock procession in the theatre the actor who was playing Vespasian's corpse sat up and asked how

147

much the funeral was costing the treasury. "Ten million sesterces," was the reply. "So give me a hundred thousand," he says, "and throw me in the Tiber." The crowd roared with delight, and I confess I was among them, despite the skit's impiousness. Really, our poor emperor was barely cold.

I have not heard from you in some weeks and am growing concerned. I trust your health continues to improve. Please reply when you can.

I had occasion to see Drusus' tutor the other day. He stopped by to inform us of his presence in Rome and to visit with Marcus. I gather that his stepmother is in serious condition and is not expected to live for too many days. Camillus seems to be bearing up as well as can be expected, although he is decidedly melancholy. What an appealing young man he is! I hope you won't consider it an impertinence to ask, but I have often wondered if there is anything between you two.

I have learned through Maria (Sabina's converted slave who is part of the Nazarene congregation here) that he attends worship service with them on a regular basis. Through her I have also discovered more about the sect. It seems that they are convinced that the end of the world is imminent, or at least that it will occur in their lifetime. They claim that this rabbi of theirs prophecied before his crucifixion that before the last man who had seen him in the flesh had died he would reappear among them and usher in the Kingdom of God. This event must now be very near, they reason, for the last of those they call "apostles" (those who knew him in the flesh) are of great age.

Through Maria, Sabina learned of a composition receiving wide circulation among them entitled "The Revelation of John" wherein all this is set forth. I had Marcus obtain a copy for me and perused it. It was apparently written nine years ago, when Titus was beseiging Jerusalem. Frankly, it struck me as little more than a propaganda document of the Jewish Zealots, and a rather violent one at that. It prophecies a final duel between Rome and Jerusalem in which the latter will be the victor. Our capital, you might be interested to learn, is treated to some rather unfavorable epithets: we are Babylon the Great squatting on our seven hills, "mother of harlots and abomination of the earth," the "great whore with whom the Kings of the world have committed fornication."

It also prophecies that the rabbi Jesus will reappear in the flesh and Rome will be overthrown. All believers who have died through persecution will then be raised from the dead, but unbelievers will remain dead for the next thousand years, during which the "righteous" will reign in glory. At the end of this thousand years, another war will somehow break out, at which time the rebels will be cast into a lake of fire and brimstone and the dead resurrected and judged. The "unrighteous" will be cast permanently into the fiery lake, while the believers shall "know death no more." Instead, they will live eternally in the new Jerusalem, to which all nations will (naturally) pay homage.

This strange polemic, whose language is full of violence and excess, seems to me a transparent attempt of the Zealots to compensate themselves psychologically for their military defeat. It reminded me of the way a child engages in vindictive fantasies in order to make himself feel better after being reprimanded by an adult. It is a pathetic document, but at the same time rather hateful. It will do the Christian cause here little good, or the Jews either, for that matter. Believing in strange gods is one thing, but talk of overthrowing the state, as this pamphlet does, is sedition. I could not help thinking that if the Nazarenes are not careful they may soon find themselves back in the arena, where so many died in Nero's time.

I would like to have questioned Camillus about this tract (I cannot believe he subscribes to such things), but alas, after a brief interview with Marcus he took his leave. He is much grieved by his mother's illness; it was not a time for disputation.

Please let me hear from you soon. My cordial regards to Drusus and Lucilla, and of course to Propertius. How is the new production coming?

Affectionately,
Aemelia

August 5

I dreamed last night I gave birth to his child. I was in a large galley that was rolling with the waves in long, slow movements. Camillus was beside me, holding my hand, but I was oblivious to anything but the tremendous force that was pushing me from inside out. There was no pain, only immense effort, and the consciousness of the irrestible power of which my body was the instrument.

And then the child was born, a beautiful boy with dark curly hair, already, to my astonishment, about one year old. We were not on a boat now but on land; the child was pursuing a butterfly through a maze of flowers at the foot of the mountain. Camillus gave chase, and the two romped and tumbled in the sunlight. I watched them, lying on a small mound of earth, overcome with love. But it occurred to me that I had become invisible. I was there, watching them, but at the same time not there. They could not see me. I stretched out my arms to them, but they remained empty. When I awoke my face was wet with tears.

The vision has haunted me throughout the day, evoking grief but somehow touching also the wellsprings of hope. As though even in death I have yet brought forth new life.

August 6

There was a frightening earthquake this afternoon when I was visiting Lucilla. She lives in the outskirts of the city, so the tremors were not as severe as in the city itself. Nevertheless they so disturbed me I left precipitously, anxious to make sure everything was all right in our quarter. Fortunately there were no injuries and no damage to the villa, although there was considerable rubble in some of the streets I passed through.

Safely back within my own walls, the terror of it comes back. Throughout the morning I was afflicted with an intense feeling of dread, a sense of knowing in advance that something dreadful was to come. I even felt, irrationally, for the sixty seconds the tremors lasted, as if my foreknowledge had somehow contributed to what happened. The statuary swayed on the pedestals, the cups on the table rattled and slid. I clutched Lucilla's hand and she mine. We sat that way, rigid with anticipation, our fear mirrored in each others' eyes. When it was over she giggled in relief and poured us more wine.

Which for once I did not begrudge her. We embraced hastily and I started to leave, but at the gate she stopped me and did something I found touching. She reached out and hugged me, this time with genuine emotion. "Don't go on holding yourself apart from me, mother," she whispered. "Whatever I am I am your daughter, and I love you," words of such rare feeling for Lucilla I was taken by surprise, disoriented as I was by the danger we had just been through.

The entire afternoon was unusual, perhaps because I consented to drink the wine unwatered. She had purchased and chilled an excellent bottle of falerian, which she served with oysters and salad. She was in high spirits, and for once tried to suppress her egotism and express concern for the rest of the family. She apologized for having caused bad feeling among us ("I know I have disappointed you, mother") but assured me that her feelings for Cornelius were genuine and not a thing of the moment. When I asked if she was continuing to see him, she replied "of course," adding that they met frequently at the baths. She assured me, however, that it was all chaste and proper.

"And Flavius?"

"It is with his consent."

It was all I could do to refrain from expressing my envy. It came upon me to ask her to speak of Cornelius and describe to me the intimate details of their affair but needless to say I did not. I felt very warmly toward her, however (the wine?), realizing I was hardly in a position any longer to pose as a moralist. She was in a playful mood, and her kittenish ways affected me as they did when she was a child.

She is a lovely young woman actually, or would be if she didn't insist on wearing so much makeup and doing her hair in those outlandish hair styles.

I asked her at one point if she knew anything of the religion of Isis. She looked at me quizzically and answered that she had seen me in the crowd at the dedication ceremonies and had wondered at my presence. "I myself went out of curiosity to see the procession," she explained. "I care little for the mysteries of the faith. Don't tell me you are thinking of becoming a devotee of Isis, mother?"

She might as well have added "at your age," for that was what she implied. I flushed and responded tartly that of course I did not, but that I saw no reason why she should speak so disparagingly of something she apparently knew little of. "Isis commands many followers, including some in the highest society," I told her.

"Really?" she replied, adding that she had little interest in such things. I started to laugh at this, for what goes on in the court is very much on her mind, but she explained that she had no use for any gods, she was too busy, and too happy, she added, if truth were known. She expressed the wish that I was also—"happy, I mean."

I wondered for an instant how much she knew, or suspected. For all I know my feelings about Camillus are written on my face. "Perhaps as you get older, you will hold happiness of less account," I answered perfunctorily, but then I was ashamed of my hypocrisy and apologized for having been so upset when she first told me her intentions of leaving Flavius. She accepted my apology, and we smiled at each other in a sort of reconciliation. One of the slave women came in at that point to report some trouble in the kitchen. Lucilla left the room; she had just come back when the ground began shaking beneath our feet.

What was going through her mind as we sat there clutching each others' hands? Was she thinking of Cornelius? What dominated my own thoughts was that if I should die I would never see Camillus again. The dream the night before of seeing him playing with our son clutched at my heart; I could hardly restrain myself from crying out his name.

The quake today was more severe than the one last month. It is childish susperstition to think in terms of three's, I know, but I am convinced there will be another, even more destructive, that these upheavals are warnings given us by the earth. But what are we do to, abandon our homes and flee? Where would we go, and for how long? The warning, if such it be, is too vague, the time of its realization too indefinite. It is not a signal one can rationally act on, for no immediate threat is visible. It therefore does not issue in action but a state of continuous dull alarm, a queasy feeling not unlike bad conscience.

Drusus seemed undisturbed by the event. Indeed, he seemed actually thrilled. Propertius tells me there was no damage to the theatre.

August 7

A note has come from him at last, saying that the doctors have given up hope for his mother. She has only a few days to live. My heart goes out to him in pity for his grief, yet a part of me also, wickedly, exults. When she dies, he will come to me.

To make the time pass more quickly, I visited the theatre yesterday and watched a rehearsal of *Octavia*. It is an odd play; despite its contemporary theme I cannot see that it will be popular. There is too much declamation, which to my mood sounded like bombast. The pathos of Octavia's plight failed to move me, and the actor who played Nero seemed to me to grossly exaggerate his gestures. To be sure, the real Nero was frequently a drunken fool, but this actor plays him purely as a buffoon, which sits ill with the tragic tone of the drama and demeans, I think, Octavia's death.

I didn't voice these criticisms to Propertius. He is intensely involved with the production, quite as if it were his child. Under the circumstances it would have been cruel to point out its deformities.

I have become addicted to daydreaming. I wander about the villa and gardens like a ghost haunting myself. Lovesickness: always before I have thought of the word as a foreign metaphor.

I have given up seeking a cure in philosophy, turning to it now only in search of distraction. I have been reading the work of Epicurus, whose discourses I borrowed on my last visit to Stabiae. Most of what I read leaves me untouched (I frequently fade off into cloudy dreams, or into the vacant space between words), but every now and then I come across a line or a phrase that stirs a response and in a spasm of discipline I copy it down:

"For most men rest is stagnation and activity madness."

"Dreams have no divine character, nor any prophetic force, but originate merely from the influx of images."

"We must not violate nature but obey her; and we shall obey her if we fulfill our necessary desires, including the physical—provided they bring no harm."

"Against all else it is possible to provide security, but as against death all of us mortals alike dwell in an unfortified city."

"Vain is the word of a philospher which does not heal the suffering of man. For just as there is no profit in medicine if it does not expel the diseases of the body, so there is no profit in philosophy either if it does not expel the suffering of the mind."

Alas, for me it does not. All the study of philosophy seems to have done is to make me more aware how unattainable the state of mind he recommends is. It has added another dimension to my melancholy, another awareness of failure.

August 9

Dreams may be "nothing but an influx of images," but where do the images come from, and why do they appear in such peculiar combinations? I was flooded with dreams again last night, although only two remain with me. The first was "ordinary," the second so intense that when I awoke I remained for a long time disoriented and uncertain of my senses.

In the first I was in the necropolis on the outskirts of the city, visiting my father's tomb. (In reality he is buried in Rome, of course, not here.) I reached into my basket to retrieve the flowers I had brought as an offering but my fingers encountered a small wooden object instead. When I drew it out I saw with surprise that it was a miniature carved phallus, much like the one I encountered the other day on the knocker of a wineshop in the city. Embarrassed, I threw it into the bushes, but as I did I perceived with astonishment that my hand had been cut off at the wrist. There was only a stump with smooth skin growing over the places where the fingers should have been. The odd thing was that I accepted the rightness of this amputation; it was as if I understood that my behaviour had brought dishonour to my father's grave and that for this breach the gods had punished me.

The second dream followed the first after a confused sequence that I do not remember. In this one I was not an actor at all, only a presence observing the scene.

Initially I saw nothing but a barren plain. There was no growth anywhere, only outcroppings of rock and rubble pocketed with black sand that lay elsewhere in mounds and small hills. The landscape was entirely unfamiliar except for the bay in the distance and the mountain. But the mountain had changed; there were two humps now instead of one, and it seemed to have shrunk in height. "Perhaps the emptiness of the landscape makes the proportions seem different," I thought, and then noticed a figure in the distance, walking down the road with the aid of a staff. It was an old man, wearing nothing but a loincloth, his body deeply tanned from the sun.

He left the road and climbed to the top of one of the mounds of rubble. There he began digging, moving the rocks and sifting the earth with his hands. There was a dogged patience to his labors which fascinated me; I was curious what he sought to uncover. I moved closer and saw that he had partially unearthed a stone pillar resembling the one at the base of the sundial in the Forum, but he ignored this and pursued his digging. The hole grew wider and deeper as he dug, until he was standing in it up to his waist. He struck something with his staff and knelt to examine it, pushing the dirt aside to uncover its form.

156

At that point I understood. I didn't need to look to know what the object was: it was the skeleton of a woman, sheltering in her arms a dead child.

The old man gave a cry and bent to touch the bones and I saw that his eyes were filled with tears. I saw also that it was Camillus. The shock of this precipitated me back into consciousness.

"Dreams have no divine character." He who can be so sure must not have experienced many of them, or at least none of this kind. Epictetus denies that there are gods who speak to us through dreams, or voices that foretell the future. I can accept the first but not the second. There may be no gods, but there is something, some dimension of reality different from the one we habitually know that dreams are connected with. I am willing to say that the dream of the necropolis resulted from an "influx of images," a rearrangement, albeit a mystifying one, of objects and thoughts I have recently encountered (I was thinking again of my father's death the other afternoon), but the second dream seems to me to bear witness to another world. Whether this world exists apart from my own consciousness I have no way of judging, but there is a certainty, a total conviction in these "special" dreams that I cannot disavow. I am utterly positive at the time I am dreaming that what I am experiencing is not a dream, whereas on other occasions I know, either in the dream itself or immediately upon waking, that the experience is only the product of imagination.

Perhaps these are the dreams the mad have; perhaps my sense of certainty is a symptom of that.

One difference between now and two months ago is that I no longer fear such dreams. They may be part of my "illness," perhaps even part of my cure, but in any case they are not subject to the will's control.

Far from strengthening my will, Eutarchus' therapeutic program seems to have had the opposite result.

There is some other will that my mind knows not that is living through me now, interweaving my soul with Camillus'. I cannot resist it. I choose not to.

August 11

I was waiting in the garden when he came. At the sight of him each of my senses quickened to life in separate rejoicings. Fortunately I had thought to bring my needlework with me so my hands would be occupied; otherwise I feared I would not be able to prevent myself from throwing my arms about his neck and clinging to him like one possessed. We did not touch in greeting but the love and joy in his eyes when he saw me was unmistakable. His countenance darkened, however, as he took his seat beside me. I remembered his grief and felt ashamed.

He was pale, with dark hollows under his eyes. Clearly he was exhausted from the journey and the long struggle that preceded it. I asked him about his mother's death and he answered, with long pauses between his sentences, that although it had been painful she had met it with courage. She had not given in to her suffering, refusing the concoctions the physicians had prepared until the very end. Shortly before she died she had said something that hurt him, something that seemed to cause him as much grief as the death itself. I could see that his pain was still raw and that he was struggling to come to terms with it. I longed to reach out and hold him, but let him talk instead.

"I have not told you much about my adopted parents' religious beliefs," he said. "My father is of the Hebrew faith, but my mother was a Roman, and as far as I know had no faith at all. She had known of my conversion to Christianity for years but made it clear to me that she was not interested in discussing it. It was therefore all the more

158

surprising when she asked me one night, a week before she died, to explain my beliefs. I did my best for the next several nights to describe my faith and why I had adopted it; I read her stories of our rabbi's teachings which I hoped would please her. I hoped, you see, that Christ's words would penetrate her heart, that I would serve as the instrument of her conversion; I wanted very badly for her to understand my beliefs and share them, and for a time I was convinced that she did. But I was wrong.

"The doctors, who could no longer alleviate her pain, had been urging her for several days to drink of the cup. On the fourth day she consented, but shortly before she did she turned to me with an expression in her eyes that haunts me still. It was as if she was already seeing me from another world, one that was indifferent to ours. Her voice was low, she was very weak, but I heard her words distinctly. "My son," she said, "it is false, this light of yours: the Messiah you believe in is of your own imagining."

He leaned forward, holding his head in his hands. "She did not have the strength to say more, although I felt at the time she wanted to. She closed her eyes, and a few minutes later, without looking at me, she asked for the cup.

"When she had drunk of it she lay back among her pillows. Then, as if taking pity on me, she took my hand. I held it for what seemed a long time, until I sensed that she could no longer feel. To my shame all I could think was that she was gone, and although she loved me her last words were to deny my faith, as if what was most important to her was to destroy it. She did not succeed, but why should she have wanted to, Claudia? I do not understand it. In the name of what value does a mother with her dying words seek to persuade her son that his faith is an illusion?"

I was as puzzled as he by this deathbed utterance, which struck me as extraordinary. But I also thought it oddly courageous. "Perhaps the Roman value of truth,

159

Camillus," I ventured.

"Truth," he echoed bitterly, "the truth of so-called reason, of inner speech rather than inner light. It is a truth of dust and ashes."

His bitterness surprised me, as did my own angry response. "I should not dismiss your mother's words so quickly if I were you," I said. "I don't know why she spoke to you as she did, I too think it is unkind, but is there not another way to look at it? She may have meant to help you, Camillus, not to cause you pain. Perhaps she was speaking as a woman as well as a Roman, and in calling your Christ an illusion she was trying to call you back to the world of flesh and blood. That seems to me entirely natural: what mother wants her son to turn his face from the life she gave him? Perhaps she saw your religion as a denial of life, in which case she was right to resent it."

He looked up at me in mute bewilderment; I had spoken more sharply than I intended. Hie eyes searched mine, groping for understanding. "Is that how my beliefs appear to you?" he asked, with such pain in his voice it caught my heart.

He turned away, but I saw that tears had filled his eyes and were rolling unheeded down his cheeks. It was like watching a statue bleed, so pale and abstracted he seemed. "Camillus, my beautiful Camillus," I said, drawing him to me, and to my joy he did not resist but pressed his dear head to my body and circled my waist with his arms. I held him as one would a child, rocking him, soothing. Never have I felt for my children such a storm of tenderness as came over me when cradling him like this, but the ecstasy was brief; the same flood that was sweeping through me coursed through him also, I know it, but he stiffened and drew away. "Forgive me," he muttered, shivering, "we cannot, I must not." He pulled his robe around him and stood up. "We cannot become lovers," he repeated distractedly, "I came here to tell you that.

Forgive me, I wish I could explain, but what I've come to tell you is that love such as ours is sinful. God may be an illusion but sin is not. Do not flinch, Claudia, at the word; I know it is alien, but it is not false. Don't you see? Sin is the refusal to follow what one knows in one's soul to be right. Happiness cannot come from something that brings pain to another. We do not exist in isolation; when we bring grief to others we bring grief to ourselves. That is what our Lord meant when he said 'He who harms the least of these has done it unto me also.' We cannot inflict pain on your husband, we have no right."

It was wrong of me to flare up, given his state of mourning, but his words exasperated me. "It is nonsense to think one can go through life without harming anyone," I retorted, "and for that matter, what of my pain? How do you know I am not 'the least of these' that your rabbi was referring to? How is my pain to be weighed in the balance with Propertius', or with your own, Camillus, or are we to be left out of account? Speak the truth, please, and do not hide behind this religion. It seems to me that what you are fleeing is not sin but the pleasure of the senses, and that I cannot understand. Is it that you prefer suffering? As if there isn't enough of that in the world already, as if we should add to it!" I paused for an instant, but when he made no answer I rushed on. "This god of yours is unworthy if he wishes us to suffer; he is also contradictory, for it was he who commanded us to love. I do not understand why it should be hedged about. 'Love him and love his commandments'—isn't that what he said? Where in those commandments is it written that we should love only through the soul? If he is as you believe the Creator of all things, it is he who created desire: surely he cannot have meant it to be frustrated and despised? Why should I accept a god who cares only for the spirit world and denies what he has created? The created world is of the flesh."

His response to this outburst was a wan smile, as

if he had heard such arguments and could easily answer them if argument was the purpose; but of course it was not. Abashed and belatedly ashamed, I apologized, begging him not to leave. I would not venture to touch him or argue against his religion again, I promised, I would respect it utterly.

I suppose I would have gone on with such promises forever but his hand stopped my mouth. "Hush," he said tenderly, "you must not say what you don't believe, and you must not cry," for I had broken down in tears. And then we were in each other's arms, and this time there was no resistance. He came with me to my rooms, and all night long we lay in each other's arms, sleeping, waking to pay homage to Eros, slipping in and out of the world of dream.

Just before dawn, thinking I was asleep, he stole from the bed. When I sat up and called his name, he came back and embraced me. "You will not leave me?" I asked. "You will not run away?"

"No," he murmured, kissing me.

"And is it still a sin?"

He kissed me again on the forehead. "Hush," he said, "we will not quarrel over a word."

He has promised not to leave me; at the moment that is all I care about. I will accept whatever he asks, even a chaste relationship, if that is his wish. Perhaps it would be possible now.

Ah, what self-deception, as if desire will not prompt me again to tempt him! To keep from touching him I would have to cut off my hands.

Yet I cannot imagine Camillus apart from his faith. It is that which causes me anguish, not the thought of Propertius or Drusus or the violation of my marriage vows. I am haunted by the idea that by loving me he will be somehow diminished, separated from his strength, that his violated conscience will torment him. It is horrible to think that through me he shall suffer. I can only pray (to whom? to Isis?) that I am not wrong, and that he does not come to see me so.

August 22

Dear Clio,

I have much to relate and little time, since I am to leave soon for Alexandria.

How strange that sounds, even to my own ears. Even stranger to realize that I do not know when or if I shall be returning.

I have asked for and received Propertius' consent to a divorce. I will be living with Camillus in Alexandria, on terms yet to be defined. He is already there, with Drusus. They left yesterday.

Perhaps I should relate the events of the past weeks in order. After I read the pamphlet you sent me on the sayings of Paul I confronted Camillus with it. We talked about your objections to Christianity and he defended it by offering a different interpretation of the text. I don't quite remember now how it happened, but at some point I confessed my love for him. I tried at the same time to let him know I would respect his freedom and that our relations need not be physical, but he was deeply upset. I could see, despite his denials, that he loved and wanted me as much as I him but his faith would not permit him to act.

The following day he left for Rome. He had recently learned that his mother was ill, but the real reason for his precipitous flight, I am sure, was that he feared what would happen if he stayed.

Ah, Clio, it was as if my confession cleaved him in two. I genuinely believe he knew nothing of my feelings until that moment, nor of his own. Now he was torn with self-doubt, possessed of two voices, not one, with no way to judge which should be followed: a condition I know

163

only too well. I hated myself for having introduced such torment into his world; when I saw his confusion I sank into despair. Strange, isn't it, how sometimes such states provoke second sight. I understood how great a threat Eros is to the rational self, perhaps even more than to the soul. With the spirit Eros is oddly allied, but it threatens to turn reason against itself, as it did with Camillus: it threatens madness, loss of control, which men fear as much if not more than death.

Before he left Camillus wrote me a letter describing his confusion and apologizing for his cowardice. He stayed in Rome for almost two weeks at his mother's bedside. Her last words, curiously, were to oppose his faith, saying that his Messiah was illusory, a gesture which greatly disturbed him. After the funeral he returned here, wounded doubly by grief and by his mother's inexplicable opposition to his beliefs. In such state his need for me at last overcame his scruples and he came to my bed.

Our lovemaking was everything I have longed for, but it was not, as I'm sure I don't have to tell you, unmixed with pain. We spent three days together, during which time I could see how worried he was over his betrayal of Propertius and his violation of his oath of chastity. I too was struggling, with anguish of my own. Despite this, illogical as it may sound, we were happy. There were many hours when we soared free, certain of our innocence, but we must have flown too high, for the scorpion guarding the sun took his revenge and delivered a sting that tumbled us back to earth. (Phaethon—do you remember speaking of this tale once at the villa?)

Watching Camillus battle his conscience, there were times when I dissolved in pity for him and would have given anything to give him back, intact, his faith. When we were together he would swear that his love for me was all that mattered, but it is far from being that simple. I do not know what will be the outcome of our

164

struggle, Clio, I fear that in Alexandria I may convert to his faith, or consent to live celibate, as brother and sister, if for no other reason than to ease his pain. I love him more than I have ever loved anyone in my life, and that is why I am following him to the East . . .

Forgive me, I am telling this poorly; I am sure you must be confused. Camillus and I never talked in specific terms of the future. We never made plans, as if knowing in advance their futility.

On the fourth day of his return the weather turned unseasonably cold. A clammy wind blew from the sea, and the light of the sky seemed oddly dim, even though there were no clouds visible. Drusus was taken with a chill and began coughing. I put him to bed immediately and sent for Eutarchus, but by the time he arrived it was clear Drusus' lungs were seriously affected: I glimpsed the bloodstained linen and was gripped by fear. The conviction that his death was imminent took possession of me; I felt my own death near, as if we would die together, but after a careful examination Eutarchus declared that although there had been a hemorrhage, it was slight. He insisted there was no immediate danger but advised strongly that my son be removed to a drier climate as soon as possible. He suggested Alexandria, to which Propertius gave his assent, reassuring me with a tenderness that compounded my guilt. Preparations were made for Camillus, Drusus and myself to leave by ship in two days' time.

The night before we were to sail I tried to compose a letter explaining my love for Camillus and asking Propertius for a divorce, but every draft I composed was inadequate to express what I felt. By the time morning came I was in the grip of fatality. I accompanied Camillus and Drusus to the dock, but did not tell them that I was not going with them, not knowing myself until the last minute that I would stay behind. I embraced Drusus, promising

165

to be with him soon.   Then I embraced Camillus, whose eyes, when he understood I was staying behind, were filled with concern.   "I must tell Propertius in person," I pleaded, "then I will follow you. Have no fear that I will not join you; I love you, I have given you my son." Wrenching myself away, I stumbled across the dock and through the gates to the city.

Back home, I went immediately to speak to Propertius. My confession shocked him. His face went white, as if he had been suddenly drained of life, making me think for a moment he had had a heart attack. I couldn't believe that what I had said should take him so by surprise. Surely my love for Camillus must have been apparent these past weeks, yet he was as stunned as if I had told him that the laws of mathematics no longer held or that the forces of nature had been suspended.

My fears that he would be hurt were justified, but for the wrong reasons: my words did not wound his heart so much as his intellect. My saying that I had rejected him for another did not disturb his pride or his sense of manhood, as I had feared, but his trust in his ability to make judgements. He had apparently believed without question that my commitment to our marriage vows was as unwavering as his; his entire sense of security, he claimed, had been grounded in trust in my loyalty. I was frankly astonished. Loyalty to what? I thought angrily—to the concept of marriage, to some abstract idea of virtue? I was offended that he could have been so blind to all the changes taking place in me. Then I thought for shame, you do your best to deceive the poor man and then outrageously blame him for not piercing your disguise: you are despicable.

He turned away so that I should not see his efforts to compose himself. When he again faced me he looked suddenly old, as if he had aged years in a few moments. His voice was calm and steady, almost fatherly, despite his grief. He told me that although it was in his own interest to ask me to stay, that he had no wish to end our marriage, that he loved me and wanted to spend the rest of his days with me, he did not believe anyone had the right to "interfere with another's choice." He was grateful, he said, that I had not left with Camillus but had stayed behind to tell him my decision in person. If I was certain I was not mistaken in my affections I should go: my place was with the man I loved.

My eyes filled with tears when he said this. He saw them and shook his head gently, as if to forbid me. His own eyes were clear. As, no doubt, is his conscience.

Ah Clio, how sad it is that even now, in the midst of my shame and pity, I cannot refrain from scorn.

He asked me to write to him from Alexandria when my mind was settled and the crisis with Drusus had passed. If at that time I wished a divorce, he told me, he would make no objection. We will decide later whether Drusus will stay on in the east or return to live here in Pompeii; such considerations will depend on his health. I am to leave the day after tomorrow, when the next ship sails.

It is done, it is accomplished, but I am numb to either relief or joy. I am conscious of nothing but immense distance, as if I am a spectator at some unusual exhibition. I feel becalmed, removed, possessed of a strange abstracted fatalism. It is as if I am awaiting my doom, almost, though the comparison is melodramatic, like a criminal awaiting execution. Yet I love him, Clio. Some of my dread may be illness, or prompted by my fear of embarking on a journey to a world I do not know; some of it is genuine anxiety that what I treasure in Camillus either has been or will be destroyed by his love for me. The victory of the flesh I accomplished under your counsel seems at this point a Pyrrhic one.

I have a further confession: if it is ordained that there is to be a contest between us, I would rather his side win than see him broken. I can hear you accusing me of submissiveness for this, but I can't help thinking that the god in whom Camillus has put his faith represents a new force in the world that is a force of liberation. The ideal of equality espoused by the Christians may never be realized, but surely any movement toward it is in a positive direction.

As you can see, I have not yet found a path out of confusion. The dialogue, however, is far from over. I have promised to visit a Christian community when I am in Alexandria; who knows what I shall find? I shall also visit the Temple of Isis, and make Camillus go with me. Alexandria is, after all, Her capital.

I will write to you again as soon as I am settled. I do not want to lose touch with you even though in future there may be greater distance between us.

Pray for me, if you do such things.

As ever,
Claudia

August 23

I should not be sitting here with this diary. The ship leaves in the morning, and I have yet to write to Lucilla.

I had another vivid dream last night. In it I entered a strange, desolate, apparently uninhabited city. I wandered about the deserted streets until I came to a square where an old woman was sitting in front of a stall containing jumbled pieces of cloth and jewelry of the sort most people throw away. I asked what city this was and why it was deserted. In answer I was told that many people had lived here before the wars. When I asked what wars, she shrugged. "Religious wars," she said, "they killed each other over the name of God." She spoke without looking up, her eyes fixed on her wares.

It seemed to me she was afraid of me, as if she thought me one of the intolerant. "I have no beliefs myself," I said, thinking to reassure her. "That's not good," she answered. "Your best protection is to possess a belief of some kind. Sometimes they respect it, sometimes not, but in my experience it's those who have a picture in their heads of how they think the world should be that are the ones who survive."

When I looked at her, mystified, she pulled out an old locket from among the jumble she was sorting and handed it to me. "Here," she said, "there's a picture in this." I took the trinket from her and pressed the latch, but it didn't open. I pressed it again and the top flew up with a snap. The locket, however, was empty; there was nothing in it. I showed it to the old woman, who responded rudely. "It's there, you're not looking," she said with contempt. The locket dropped from my hand. I stooped to search for it and found it beneath one of the folds of my skirt, but when I stood up the old woman was gone. I looked for her but couldn't find her.

After I woke I lay for a long time watching the dawn lighten the objects in my room. My thoughts kept going back to the woman in the dream and the way I had sought to persuade her that I have no belief. It is true, I thought: I can believe in neither Christ nor Isis. Both are alien to me, products of a foreign soil. The gods of my own country are equally unreal; the more emperors we deify the more absurd and unacceptable our beliefs appear. Rome is rich in philosophers and does not lack models of human virtue, but wise as our thinkers may be, Camillus is right in saying that their counsels do not penetrate the heart.

The night before Drusus' hemorrhage Camillus and I went for a long walk by the sea, outside the gates of the city. I confessed to him my nightmares and fears, and my recurrent premonitions of catastrophe. He listened in sympathy, making no attempt to pass it off as illness. He did not understand the nature of dreams any more than anyone else, he said, although many Nazarenes believed that a catastrophe similar to what I had envisioned was very near. "None of us can be certain of the future," he told me, "but whether the cataclysm which many see approaching comes to pass or not it seems to me perilous to let oneself be determined by such ideas. To think that way is only another mode of selfishness. I can not believe that the Christ to whom I have pledged my soul would visit wholesale destruction upon his creation, even if it has fallen into error. I do not believe he is capable of allowing such evil; if he is, then life is a mockery."

"Do you not believe in an afterlife then, Camillus," I asked, "in the doctrine of hell, the casting of the unrighteous into a lake of fire?"

I was referring to the tract circulating in Rome. He replied that he did not believe such visions, that the hell of which his master spoke was of this world, consisting of the suffering attendant upon the denial of God, of knowing oneself separate from him, and unworthy.

Which is how he made me feel many times, without intending it.

I am one of the blinded he referred to when he spoke once of the fallen human world. "It is as if we have lost our sight," he said. "For the most part we exist in despair, without being aware of it. Because we don't realize fully who we are we inextricably entangle ourselves in error; it films our eyes and keeps us from seeing that paradise is all around, that it exists within . . . ."

He seems very beautiful to me when he speaks of his religion. Shall I ever know his god, I wonder, except through him, through love of his physical being? I feel as if I am blaspheming when he speaks of his Christ, for what I see in imagination is not the face of a god but Camillus' face as he bent over me in my bedchamber, the feel of his body inside mine . . . .

170

Drusus will live, I am certain of it; for reasons I can't explain I am persuaded that the gods will protect him. Lucilla too will find her way. Perhaps it is my pity for Propertius that makes me so remote and disbelieving. I feel as if I am sleepwalking, as if the journey tomorrow and the future is a dream.

I look around my room for the last time, certain such familiar sights will always be with me. Nonetheless I try to fix them in memory, the draperies, the bed on which Camillus and I made love, my dressing table, my brushes, my mother's Syrian vase. They are objects of no value apart from the memories I have invested them with, yet I shall be sorry to abandon them.

And to abandon these scrolls, which have offered such solace these past weeks. I must ask Scribonia to burn them after I leave; I cannot do it myself.

What do I retrieve from my nights of study, what pearls will accompany me as spiritual dowry? I open my scroll of Epictetus at random. He advises me to compose my spirits: "Ever seeking peace outside you, you will never be able to find it, for you seek it where it is not . . . ."

Curious words for someone setting out on a journey; I wonder what Camillus will say to them.

I shall sleep now: at dawn a new chapter begins.

Translator's Note

On August 24 A.D. 79, Mount Vesuvius, which had remained quiescent for over two hundred years, erupted without warning, obliterating the city of Pompeii. Some of the inhabitants escaped by sea, but the majority of the population succumbed to poisonous gasses or were crushed by falling masonry. Within two days all who remained within the city gates were buried in molten lava and ash. Most of the major buildings, including both theatres, were destroyed by earthquake; the newly restored Iseum perished by flames.

The historian Pliny the Younger, vacationing at the time at Stabiae across the Bay, wrote of the catastrophe to his friend Tacitus. His description of the events of August 24 and 25 are frighteningingly vivid, and may remind contemporary readers of a similar threat present in our own time:

"My uncle was stationed at Misenum, in active command of the fleet. . . . In the early afternoon, my mother drew his attention to a cloud of unusual size and appearance. It was not clear from which mountain the cloud was rising—it was afterwards known to be Vesuvius. Its general appearance was rather like that of a tree, and particularly a pine, for it rose to a great height on a trunk, splitting into branches. Sometimes it looked white, sometimes blotched and dirty, depending on whether it was carrying off soil or ashes.

"The phenomenon aroused my uncle's scientific curiosity and he decided to examine it more closely. We hurried to the place which everyone else was fleeing, sailing straight into danger. Ashes were already falling, hotter and thicker as the ships drew near, followed by bits of pumice and blackened stones; then suddenly we were in shallow water and the shore was blocked by debris from the mountain. Meanwhile broad sheets of fire and leaping flames blazed at several points, their glare emphasized by the darkness...

"Elsewhere day was dawning, but for those on the beach it was still the blackest night. The smell of sulphur which was a warning of the nearness of danger drove everyone to flight. My uncle stood leaning on two slaves, and suddenly collapsed dead. . . .

"By now it was dawn, but the light was still dim and faint. The buildings around us were already tottering. I looked behind me to see a thick black cloud coming up fast, spreading over the earth like a flood. 'Let us leave the road while we can still see,' I said to my mother. We could hear women crying, children howling, men shouting. Someone was calling out for his father, another for his son, another for his wife; they were trying to recognize each other by the sounds of their voices. There were those who prayed for death in their terror of dying. Many sought the aid of the gods, but still more were convinced that there were no gods left and that the universe was plunged into darkness for ever more.

"A gleam of light appeared, but we took this not for the return of daylight but as a warning of the approaching flames. Then darkness returned and the shower of ash grew heavier and thicker than before. We rose from time to time and shook off the cinders which would otherwise have crushed and buried us. I could boast that not a groan or a sigh of fear escaped me; for I was consoled by the dreadful yet comforting thought that the universe was dying with me, and I with it . . . ."

There were no skeletal remains excavated in the ruins of the Villa Propertii from which the manuscript scrolls translated here were recovered. Whether the author of the scrolls was one of those who escaped from the city by sea is not known.

Spem habemus: one hopes so.